MARY POPPINS
COMES BACK

OTHER YEARLING BOOKS YOU WILL ENJOY:

YEARLING BOOKS/YOUNG YEARLINGS/YEARLING CLASSICS are designed especially to entertain and enlighten young people. Patricia Reilly Giff, consultant to this series, received the bachelor's degree from Marymount College. She holds the master's degree in history from St. John's University, and a Professional Diploma in Reading from Hofstra University. She was a teacher and reading consultant for many years, and is the author of numerous books for young readers.

"*They saw before them their own pictured faces*"

MARY POPPINS
COMES BACK

P. L. Travers

With original illustrations by Mary Shepard

A Yearling Book

Published by
Dell Publishing
a division of
Bantam Doubleday Dell Publishing Group, Inc.
666 Fifth Avenue
New York, New York 10103

ISBN: 0-440-40418-5

Reprinted by arrangement with Harcourt Brace Jovanovich,
Publishers

Printed in the United States of America

April 1991

10 9 8 7 6 5 4 3 2 1

OPM

TO PIP, THIS KEEPSAKE

CONTENTS

ILLUSTRATIONS

ILLUSTRATIONS XV

MARY POPPINS
COMES BACK

MARY POPPINS COMES BACK

CHAPTER

I

THE KITE

IT WAS one of those mornings when everything looks very neat and bright and shiny, as though the world had been tidied up overnight.

In Cherry Tree Lane the houses blinked as their blinds went up, and the thin shadows of the cherry-trees fell in dark stripes across the sunlight. But there was no sound anywhere, except for the tingling of the Ice Cream Man's bell as he wheeled his cart up and down.

"STOP ME AND BUY ONE"

said the placard in front of the cart. And presently a Sweep came round the corner of the Lane and held up his black sweepy hand.

The Ice Cream Man went tingling up to him.

"Penny one," said the Sweep. And he stood leaning on his bundle of brushes as he licked out the Ice Cream with the tip of his tongue. When it was all gone he gently wrapped the cone in his handkerchief and put it in his pocket.

"Don't you eat cones?" said the Ice Cream Man, very surprised.

"No. I collect them!" said the Sweep. And he picked up his brushes and went in through Admiral Boom's front gate because there was no Tradesmen's Entrance.

The Ice Cream Man wheeled his cart up the Lane again and tingled, and the stripes of shadow and sunlight fell on him as he went.

"Never knew it so quiet before!" he murmured, gazing from right to left, and looking out for customers.

At that very moment a loud voice sounded from Number Seventeen. The Ice Cream Man cycled hurriedly up to the gate, hoping for an order.

"I won't stand it! I simply will not stand any more!" shouted Mr. Banks, striding angrily from the front door to the foot of the stairs and back again.

"What is it?" said Mrs. Banks anxiously, hurrying out of the dining-room. "And what is that you are kicking up and down the hall?"

Mr. Banks lunged out with his foot and something black flew half-way up the stairs.

"My hat!" he said between his teeth. "My Best Bowler Hat!"

He ran up the stairs and kicked it down again. It spun for a moment on the tiles and fell at Mrs. Banks' feet.

"Is anything wrong with it?" said Mrs. Banks, nervously. But to herself she wondered whether there was not something wrong with Mr. Banks.

"Look and see!" he roared at her.

Trembling, Mrs. Banks stooped and picked up the hat. It was covered with large, shiny, sticky patches and she noticed it had a peculiar smell.

She sniffed at the brim.

"It smells like boot-polish," she said.

"It *is* boot-polish," retorted Mr. Banks. "Robertson Ay has brushed my hat with the boot-brush—in fact, he has polished it."

Mrs. Banks' mouth fell with horror.

"I don't know what's come over this house," Mr. Banks went on. "Nothing ever goes right—hasn't for ages! Shaving water too hot, breakfast coffee too cold. And now—this!"

He snatched his hat from Mrs. Banks and caught up his bag.

"I am going!" he said. "And I don't know that I shall ever come back. I shall probably take a long sea-voyage."

Then he clapped the hat on his head, banged the front door behind him and went through the gate so quickly that he knocked over the Ice Cream Man, who had been listening to the conversation with interest.

"It's your own fault!" he said crossly. "You'd no right to be there!" And he went striding off towards the City, his polished hat shining like a jewel in the sun.

The Ice Cream Man got up carefully and, finding there were no bones broken, he sat down on the kerb, and made it up to himself by eating a large Ice Cream. . . .

"Oh, dear!" said Mrs. Banks as she heard the gate slam. "It is quite true. Nothing *does* go right nowadays. First one thing and then another. Ever since Mary Poppins left without a Word of Warning everything has gone wrong."

She sat down at the foot of the stairs and took out her handkerchief and cried into it.

And as she cried, she thought of all that had happened since that day when Mary Poppins had so suddenly and so strangely disappeared.

"Here one night and gone the next—most upsetting!" said Mrs. Banks gulping.

Nurse Green had arrived soon after and had left at the end of a week because Michael had spat at her. She was followed by Nurse Brown who went out for a walk one day and never came back. And it was not until later that they discovered that all the silver spoons had gone with her.

And after Nurse Brown came Miss Quigley, the Governess, who had to be asked to leave because she played scales for three hours every morning before breakfast and Mr. Banks did not care for music.

"And then," sobbed Mrs. Banks to her handkerchief, "there was Jane's attack of measles, and the bath-room geyser bursting and the Cherry Trees ruined by frost and——"

"If you please, m'm——!" Mrs. Banks looked up to find Mrs. Brill, the cook, at her side.

"The kitchen flue's on fire!" said Mrs. Brill gloomily.

"Oh, dear. What next?" cried Mrs. Banks. "You must tell Robertson Ay to put it out. Where is he?"

"Asleep, m'm, in the broom cupboard. And when that boy's asleep, nothing'll wake him—not if it's an Earthquake, or a regiment of Tom-toms," said Mrs. Brill, as she followed Mrs. Banks down the kitchen stairs.

Between them they managed to put out the fire but that was not the end of Mrs. Banks' troubles.

She had no sooner finished luncheon than a crash, followed by a loud thud, was heard from upstairs.

"What is it now?" Mrs. Banks rushed out to see what had happened.

"Oh, my leg, my leg!" cried Ellen, the housemaid.

She sat on the stairs, surrounded by broken china, groaning loudly.

"What is the matter with it?" said Mrs. Banks sharply.

"Broken!" said Ellen dismally, leaning against the banisters.

"Nonsense, Ellen! You've sprained your ankle, that's all!"

But Ellen only groaned again.

"My leg is broken! What will I do?" she wailed, over and over again.

At that moment the shrill cries of the Twins sounded from the nursery. They were fighting for the possession of a blue celluloid duck. Their screams rose thinly above the voices of Jane and Michael who were painting pictures on the wall and arguing as to whether a green horse should have a purple or a red tail. And through this uproar there sounded, like the steady beat of a drum, the groans of Ellen the house-maid. "My leg is broken! What shall I do?"

"This," said Mrs. Banks, rushing upstairs, "is the Last Straw!"

She helped Ellen to bed and put a cold water bandage round her ankle. Then she went up to the Nursery.

Jane and Michael rushed at her.

"It should have a red tail, shouldn't it?" demanded Michael.

"Oh, Mother! Don't let him be so stupid. No horse has a red tail, has it?"

"Well, what horse has a purple tail? Tell me that!" he screamed.

"*My* duck!" shrieked John, snatching the duck from Barbara.

"Mine, mine, mine!" cried Barbara, snatching it back again.

"Children! Children!" Mrs. Banks was wringing her hands in despair. "Be quiet or I shall Go Mad!"

There was silence for a moment as they stared at her with interest. Would she really? They wondered. And what would she be like if she did?

"Now," said Mrs. Banks. "I will *not* have this behaviour. Poor Ellen has hurt her ankle, so there is nobody to look after you. You must all go into the Park and play there till Tea-time. Jane and Michael, you must look after the little ones. John, let Barbara have the duck now and you can have it when you go to bed. Michael, you may take your new kite. Now, get your hats, all of you!"

"But I want to finish my horse——" began Michael crossly.

"Why must we go to the Park?" complained Jane. "There's nothing to do there!"

"Because," said Mrs. Banks, "I *must* have peace. And if you will go quietly and be good children there will be cocoanut cakes for tea."

And before they had time to break out again, she had put on their hats and was hurrying them down the stairs.

"Look both ways!" she called as they went through the gate, Jane pushing the Twins in the perambulator and Michael carrying his kite.

They looked to the right. There was nothing coming.

They looked to the left. Nobody there but the Ice Cream Man who was jingling his bell at the end of the Lane.

Jane hurried across.

Michael trailed after her.

"I hate this life," he said miserably to his kite. "Everything always goes wrong always."

Jane pushed the perambulator as far as the Lake. "Now," she said, "give me the duck!"

The Twins shrieked and clutched it at either end. Jane uncurled their fingers.

"Look!" she said, throwing the duck into the Lake. "Look, darlings, it's going to India!"

The duck drifted off across the water. The Twins stared at it and sobbed.

Jane ran round the Lake and caught it and sent it off again.

"Now," she said brightly, "it's off to Southampton!"

The Twins did not appear to be amused.

"Now to New York!" They wept harder than ever.

Jane flung out her hands. "Michael, what *are* we to do with them? If we give it to them they'll fight over it and if we don't they'll go on crying."

"I'll fly the Kite for them," said Michael. "Look, children, look!"

He held up the beautiful green-and-yellow Kite and began to unwind the string. The Twins eyed it tearfully and without interest. He lifted the Kite above his head and ran a little way. It flapped along the air for a moment and then collapsed hollowly on the grass.

"Try again!" said Jane encouragingly.

"You hold it up while I run," said Michael.

This time the Kite rose a little higher. But, as it floated, its long tasselled tail caught in the branches of a lime tree and the Kite dangled limply among the leaves.

The Twins howled lustily.

"Oh, dear!" said Jane. "Nothing goes right nowadays."

"Hullo, hullo, hullo! What's all this?" said a voice behind them.

They turned and saw the Park Keeper, looking very smart in his uniform and peaked cap. He was prodding up stray pieces of paper with the sharp end of his walking stick.

Jane pointed to the lime tree. The Keeper looked up. His face became very stern.

"Now, now, you're breaking the rules! We don't allow Litter here, you know—not on the ground nor in the trees neither. This won't do at all!"

"It isn't litter. It's a Kite," said Michael.

A mild, soft, foolish look came over the Keeper's face. He went up to the lime tree.

"A Kite? So it is. And I haven't flown a Kite since I was a boy!" He sprang up into the tree and came down holding the Kite tenderly under his arm.

"Now," he said excitedly, "we'll wind her up and give her a run and away she'll go!" He put out his hand for the winding stick.

Michael clutched it firmly.

"Thank you, but I want to fly it myself."

"Well, but you'll let me help, won't you?" said the Keeper humbly. "Seeing as I got it down and I haven't flown a Kite since I was a boy?"

"All right," said Michael, for he didn't want to seem unkind.

"Oh, thank you, thank you!" cried the Keeper gratefully. "Now, I take the Kite and walk ten paces down the green. And when I say 'Go!', you run. See!"

The Keeper walked away, counting his steps out loud.

"Eight, nine, ten."

He turned and raised the Kite above his head. "Go!"

Michael began to run.

"Let her out!" roared the Keeper.

Behind him Michael heard a soft flapping noise. There was a tug at the string as the winding-stick turned in his hand.

"She's afloat!" cried the Keeper.

Michael looked back. The Kite was sailing through the air, plunging steadily upwards. Higher and higher it dived, a tiny wisp of green-and-yellow bounding away into the blue. The Keeper's eyes were popping.

"I never saw such a Kite. Not even when I was a boy," he murmured, staring upwards.

A light cloud came up over the sun and puffed across the sky.

"It's coming towards the Kite," said Jane in an excited whisper.

Up and up went the tossing tail, darting through the air until it seemed but a faint dark speck on the sky. The cloud moved slowly towards it. Nearer, nearer!

"Gone!" said Michael, as the speck disappeared behind the thin grey screen.

Jane gave a little sigh. The Twins sat quietly in the perambulator. A curious stillness was upon them all. The taut string running up from Michael's hand seemed to link them all to the cloud, and the earth to the sky. They waited, holding their breaths, for the Kite to appear again.

Suddenly Jane could bear it no longer.

"Michael," she cried, "Pull it in! Pull it in!"

She laid her hand upon the tugging, quivering string.

Michael turned the stick and gave a long, strong pull. The string remained taut and steady. He pulled again, puffing and panting.

"I can't," he said. "It won't come."

"I'll help!" said Jane. "Now—pull!"

But, hard as they tugged, the string would not give and the Kite remained hidden behind the cloud.

"Let me!" said the Keeper importantly. "When I was a boy we did it this way."

And he put his hand on the string just above Jane's and gave it a short, sharp jerk. It seemed to give a little.

"Now—all together—pull!" he yelled.

The Keeper tossed off his hat, and, planting their

On sailed the curious figure, its feet neatly clearing the tops of the trees

feet firmly on the grass, Jane and Michael pulled with all their might.

"It's coming!" panted Michael.

Suddenly the string slackened and a small whirling

shape shot through the grey cloud and came floating down.

"Wind her up!" the Keeper spluttered, glancing at Michael.

But the string was already winding round the stick of its own accord.

Down, down came the Kite, turning over and over in the air, wildly dancing at the end of the jerking string.

Jane gave a little gasp.

"Something's happened!" she cried. "That's not our Kite. It's quite a different one!"

They stared.

It was quite true. The Kite was no longer green-and-yellow. It had turned colour and was now navy-blue. Down it came, tossing and bounding.

Suddenly Michael gave a shout.

"Jane! Jane! It isn't a Kite at all. It looks like— oh, it looks like——"

"Wind, Michael, wind quickly!" gasped Jane. "I can hardly wait!"

For now, above the tallest trees, the shape at the end of the string was clearly visible. There was no sign of the green-and-yellow Kite but in its place danced a figure that seemed at once strange and familiar, a figure wearing a blue coat with silver buttons and a straw hat trimmed with daisies. Tucked under its arm was an umbrella with a parrot's head for a handle, a brown carpet-bag dangled from one hand while the other held firmly to the end of the shortening string.

"Ah!" Jane gave a shout of triumph. "It *is* she!"

"I knew it!" cried Michael, his hands trembling on the winding-stick.

"Lumme!" said the Park Keeper, blinking. "Lumme!"

On sailed the curious figure, its feet neatly clearing the tops of the trees. They could see the face now and the well-known features—coal black hair, bright blue eyes and nose turned upwards like the nose of a Dutch doll. As the last length of string wound itself round the stick the figure drifted down between the lime trees and alighted primly upon the grass.

In a flash Michael dropped the stick. Away he bounded, with Jane at his heels.

"Mary Poppins, Mary Poppins!" they cried, and flung themselves upon her.

Behind them the Twins were crowing like cocks in the morning and the Park Keeper was opening and shutting his mouth as though he would like to say something but could not find the words.

"At last! At last! At last!" shouted Michael wildly, clutching at her arm, her bag, her umbrella—anything, so long as he might touch her and feel that she was really true.

"We knew you'd come back! We found the letter that said *au revoir*!" cried Jane, flinging her arms round the waist of the blue overcoat.

A satisfied smile flickered for a moment over Mary Poppins' face—up from the mouth, over the turned-up nose, into the blue eyes. But it died away swiftly.

"I'll thank you to remember," she remarked, disengaging herself from their hands, "that this is a Public Park and not a Bear Garden. Such goings on!

I might as well be at the Zoo. And where, may I ask, are your gloves?"

They fell back, fumbling in their pockets.

"Humph! Put them on, please!"

Trembling with excitement and delight, Jane and Michael stuffed their hands into the gloves and put on their hats.

Mary Poppins moved towards the perambulator. The Twins cooed happily as she strapped them in more securely and straightened the rug. Then she glanced round.

"Who put that duck in the pond?" she demanded, in that stern, haughty voice they knew so well.

"I did," said Jane. "For the Twins. He was going to New York."

"Well, take him out, then!" said Mary Poppins. "He is not going to New York—wherever that is—but Home to Tea."

And, slinging her carpet-bag over the handle of the perambulator, she began to push the Twins towards the gate.

The Park Keeper, suddenly finding his voice, blocked her way.

"See here," he said, staring. "I shall have to report this. It's against the Regulations. Coming down out of the sky, like that. And where from, I'd like to know, where from?"

He broke off, for Mary Poppins was eyeing him up and down in a way that made him feel he would rather be somewhere else.

"If I was a Park Keeper," she remarked, primly,

"I should put on my cap and button my coat. Excuse me."

And, haughtily waving him aside, she pushed past with the perambulator.

Blushing, the Keeper bent to pick up his hat. When he looked up again Mary Poppins and the children had disappeared through the gate of Number Seventeen Cherry Tree Lane.

He stared at the path. Then he stared up at the sky and down at the path again.

He took off his hat, scratched his head, and put it on again.

"I never saw such a thing!" he said, shakily. "Not even when I was a boy!"

And he went away muttering and looking very upset.

"Why, it's Mary Poppins!" said Mrs. Banks, as they came into the hall. "Where did *you* come from? Out of the blue?"

"Yes," began Michael joyfully, "she came down on the end——"

He stopped short for Mary Poppins had fixed him with one of her terrible looks.

"I found them in the Park, ma'am," she said, turning to Mrs. Banks, "so I brought them home!"

"Have you come to stay, then?"

"For the present, ma'am."

"But, Mary Poppins, last time you were here you left me without a Word of Warning. How do I know you won't do it again?"

"You don't, ma'am," replied Mary Poppins, calmly.
Mrs. Banks looked rather taken aback.

"But—but will you, do you think?" she asked uncertainly.

"I couldn't say, ma'am, I'm sure."

"Oh!" said Mrs. Banks, because, at the moment,
she couldn't think of anything else.

And before she had recovered from her surprise,
Mary Poppins had taken her carpet-bag and was
hurrying the children upstairs.

Mrs. Banks, gazing after them, heard the Nursery
door shut quietly. Then with a sigh of relief she ran
to the telephone.

"Mary Poppins has come back!" she said happily,
into the receiver.

"Has she, indeed?" said Mr. Banks at the other
end. "Then perhaps I will, too."

And he rang off.

Upstairs Mary Poppins was taking off her overcoat.
She hung it on a hook behind the Night-Nursery
door. Then she removed her hat and placed it neatly
on one of the bed-posts.

Jane and Michael watched the familiar movements.
Everything about her was just as it had always been.
They could hardly believe she had ever been away.

Mary Poppins bent down and opened the carpet
bag.

It was quite empty except for a large Thermometer.

"What's that for?" asked Jane curiously.

"You," said Mary Poppins.

"But I'm not ill," Jane protested. "It's two months since I had measles."

"Open!" said Mary Poppins in a voice that made Jane shut her eyes very quickly and open her mouth. The Thermometer slipped in.

"I want to know how you've been behaving since I went away," remarked Mary Poppins sternly. Then she took out the Thermometer and held it up to the light.

"Careless, thoughtless and untidy," she read out.

Jane stared.

"Humph!" said Mary Poppins, and thrust the Thermometer into Michael's mouth. He kept his lips tightly pressed upon it until she plucked it out and read,

"A very noisy, mischievous, troublesome little boy."

"I'm not," he said angrily.

For answer she thrust the Thermometer under his nose and he spelt out the large red letters.

"A-V-E-R-Y-N-O-I-S——"

"You see?" said Mary Poppins looking at him triumphantly. She opened John's mouth and popped in the Thermometer.

"Peevish and Excitable." That was John's temperature.

And when Barbara's was taken Mary Poppins read out the two words, "Thoroughly spoilt."

"Humph!" she snorted. "It's about time I came back!"

Then she popped it quickly in her own mouth, left it there for a moment, and took it out.

"A very excellent and worthy person, thoroughly reliable in every particular."

A pleased and conceited smile lit up her face as she read her temperature aloud.

"I thought so," she said, priggishly. "Now—Tea and Bed!"

It seemed to them no more than a minute before they had drunk their milk and eaten their cocoanut cakes and were in and out of the bath. As usual, everything that Mary Poppins did had the speed of electricity. Hooks and eyes rushed apart, buttons darted eagerly out of their holes, sponge and soap ran up and down like lightning, and towels dried with one rub.

Mary Poppins walked along the row of beds tucking them all in. Her starched white apron crackled and she smelt deliciously of newly-made toast.

When she came to Michael's bed she bent down, and rummaged under it for a minute. Then she carefully drew out her camp-bedstead with her possessions laid upon it in neat piles. The cake of Sunlight-soap, the toothbrush, the packet of hairpins, the bottle of scent, the small folding arm-chair and the box of throat lozenges. Also the seven flannel nightgowns, the four cotton ones, the boots, the dominoes, the two bathing-caps and the postcard album.

Jane and Michael sat up and stared.

"Where did they come from?" demanded Michael.

"I've been under my bed simply hundreds of times and I know they weren't there before."

Mary Poppins did not reply. She had begun to undress.

Jane and Michael exchanged glances. They knew it was no good asking, because Mary Poppins never explained anything.

She slipped off her starched white collar and fumbled at the clip of a chain round her neck.

"What's inside that?" enquired Michael, gazing at a small gold locket that hung on the end of the chain.

"A portrait."

"Whose?"

"You'll know when the time comes—not before," she snapped.

"When will the time come?"

"When I go."

They stared at her with startled eyes.

"But, Mary Poppins," cried Jane, "you won't ever leave us again, will you? Oh, say you won't!"

Mary Poppins glared at her.

"A nice life I'd have," she remarked, "if I spent all my days with *you!*"

"But you will stay?" persisted Jane eagerly.

Mary Poppins tossed the locket up and down on her palm.

"I'll stay till the chain breaks," she said briefly.

And popping a cotton nightgown over her head, she began to undress beneath it.

"That's all right," Michael whispered across to Jane. "I noticed the chain and it's a very strong one!"

He nodded to her reassuringly. They curled up in

their beds and lay watching Mary Poppins as she moved mysteriously beneath the tent of her night-gown. And they thought of her first arrival at Cherry Tree Lane and all the strange and astonishing things that happened afterwards; of how she had flown away on her umbrella when the wind changed; of the long weary days without her and her marvellous descent from the sky this afternoon.

Suddenly Michael remembered something.

"My Kite!" he said, sitting up in bed. "I forgot all about it! Where's my Kite?"

Mary Poppins' head came up through the neck of the nightgown.

"Kite?" she said crossly. "Which Kite? What Kite?"

"My green-and-yellow Kite with the tassels. The one you came down on, at the end of the string."

Mary Poppins stared at him. He could not tell if she was more astonished than angry, but she looked as if she was both.

And her voice when she spoke, was more awful than her look.

"Did I understand you to say that——" she repeated the words slowly, between her teeth—"that I came down from somewhere and on the end of a string?"

"But—you did!" faltered Michael. "To-day. Out of a cloud. We saw you."

"On the end of a string? Like a monkey or a spinning-top? Me, Michael Banks?"

Mary Poppins, in her fury, seemed to have grown to twice her usual size. She hovered over him in her nightgown, huge and angry, waiting for him to reply.

He clutched the bed-clothes for support.

"Don't say any more, Michael!" Jane whispered warningly across from her bed. But he had gone too far now to stop.

"Then—where's my Kite?" he said recklessly. "If you didn't come down—er, in the way I said—where's my Kite? It's not on the end of the string."

"O-ho? And I am, I suppose?" she enquired with a scoffing laugh.

He saw then that it was no good going on. He could not explain. He would have to give it up.

"N—no," he said, in a thin, small voice. "No, Mary Poppins."

She turned and snapped out the electric light.

"Your manners," she remarked tartly, "have not improved since I went away! On the end of a string, indeed! I have never been so insulted in my life. Never!"

And with a furious sweep of her arm, she turned down her bed and flounced into it, pulling the blankets tight over her head.

Michael lay very quiet, still holding his bed-clothes tightly.

"She did, though, didn't she? We saw her." He whispered presently to Jane.

But Jane did not answer. Instead, she pointed towards the Night-Nursery door.

Michael lifted his head cautiously.

Behind the door, on a hook, hung Mary Poppins' overcoat, its silver buttons gleaming in the glow of the night-light. And, dangling from the pocket, were a row of paper tassels, the tassels of a green-and-yellow Kite.

They gazed at it for a long time.

Then they nodded across to each other. They knew there was nothing to be said, for there were things about Mary Poppins they would never understand. But—she was back again. That was all that mattered. The even sound of her breathing came floating across from the camp-bed. They felt peaceful and happy and complete.

"I don't mind, Jane, if it has a purple tail," hissed Michael presently.

"No, Michael!" said Jane. "I really think a red would be better."

After that there was no sound in the nursery but the sound of five people breathing very quietly. . . .

"P-p! P-p!" went Mr. Banks' pipe.

'Click-click!" went Mrs. Banks' knitting needles.

Mr. Banks put his feet up on the study mantle-piece and snored a little.

After a while Mrs. Banks spoke.

"Do you still think of taking a long sea-voyage?" she asked.

"Er—I don't think so. I am rather a bad sailor. And my hat's all right now. I had the whole of it polished by the shoe-black at the corner and it looks as good as new. Even better. Besides, now that Mary Poppins is back, my shaving water will be just the right temperature."

Mrs. Banks smiled to herself and went on knitting.

She felt very glad that Mr. Banks was such a bad sailor and that Mary Poppins had come back.

Down in the Kitchen, Mrs. Brill was putting a fresh bandage round Ellen's ankle.

"I never thought much of her when she was here!" said Mrs. Brill, "but I must say that this has been a different house since this afternoon. As quiet as a Sunday and as neat as ninepence. I'm not sorry she's back."

"Neither am I, indeed!" said Ellen thankfully.

"And neither am I," thought Robertson Ay, listening to the conversation through the wall of the Broom-cupboard. "Now I shall have a little peace."

He settled himself comfortably on the upturned coal-scuttle and fell asleep again with his head against a broom.

But what Mary Poppins thought about it nobody ever knew for she kept her thoughts to herself and never told anyone anything. . . .

2

MISS ANDREW'S LARK

IT WAS Saturday afternoon.

In the hall of Number Seventeen, Cherry Tree Lane, Mr. Banks was busy tapping the barometer and telling Mrs. Banks what the weather was going to do.

"Moderate South wind; average temperature; local thunder; sea slight," he said. "Further outlook unsettled. Hullo—what's that?"

He broke off as a bumping, jumping, thumping noise sounded overhead.

Round the bend in the staircase Michael appeared, looking very bad-tempered and sulky as he bumped heavily down. Behind him with a Twin on each arm came Mary Poppins, pushing her knee into his back and sending him with a sharp thud from one stair to the next. Jane followed, carrying the hats.

"Well begun is half done. Down you go, please!" Mary Poppins was saying tartly.

Mr. Banks turned from the barometer and looked up as they appeared.

"Well, what's the matter with you?" he demanded.

"I don't *want* to go for a walk! I want to play with my new engine," said Michael, gulping as Mary Poppins's knee jerked him one stair lower.

"Nonsense, darling!" said Mrs. Banks. "Of course you do. Walking makes such long, strong legs."

"But I like short legs best," grumbled Michael, stumbling heavily down another stair.

"When *I* was a little boy," said Mr. Banks, "I loved going for walks. I used to walk with my Governess down to the second lamp-post and back every day. And I *never* grumbled."

Michael stood still on his stair and looked doubtfully at Mr. Banks.

"Were you *ever* a little boy?" he said, very surprised.

Mr. Banks seemed quite hurt.

"Of course I was. A sweet little boy with long yellow curls, velvet breeches and button-up boots."

"I can hardly believe it," said Michael, hurrying down the stairs of his own accord and staring up at Mr. Banks.

He simply could not imagine his Father as a little boy. It seemed to him impossible that Mr. Banks had ever been anything but six feet high, middle-aged and rather bald.

"What was the name of your Governess?" asked Jane, running downstairs after Michael. "And was she nice?"

"She was called Miss Andrew and she was a Holy Terror!"

"Hush!" said Mrs. Banks, reproachfully.

"I mean—" Mr. Banks corrected himself, "she was—er—very strict. And always right. And she loved putting everybody else in the wrong and making them feel like a worm. That's what Miss Andrew was like!"

Mr. Banks mopped his brow at the mere memory of his Governess.

Ting! Ting! Ting!

The front door bell pealed and echoed through the house.

Mr. Banks went to the door and opened it. On the step, looking very important, stood the Telegraph Boy.

"Urgent Telegram. Name of Banks. Any answer?" He handed over an orange-coloured envelope.

"If it's good news I'll give you sixpence," said Mr. Banks as he tore open the Telegram and read the message. His face grew pale.

"No answer," he said shortly.

"And no sixpence?"

"Certainly not!" said Mr. Banks bitterly. The Telegraph Boy gave him a reproachful look and went sorrowfully away.

"Oh, what is it?" asked Mrs. Banks, realising the news must be very bad. "Is somebody ill?"

"Worse than that," said Mr. Banks miserably.

"Have we lost all our money?" By this time Mrs. Banks, too, was pale and very anxious.

"Worse still! Didn't the barometer say thunder? And further outlook Unsettled? Listen!"

He smoothed out the telegram and read aloud—

"Coming to stay with you for a month. Arriving this afternoon three o'clock. Please light fire in bedroom.
EUPHEMIA ANDREW."

"Andrew? Why, that's the same name as your Governess!" said Jane.

"It *is* my Governess," said Mr. Banks, striding up and down and running his hands nervously through what was left of his hair. "Her other name is Euphemia. And she's coming to-day at three!"

He groaned loudly.

"But I don't call that bad news," said Mrs. Banks, feeling very relieved. "It will mean getting the spare room ready, of course, but I don't mind. I shall like having the dear old soul——"

"Dear old soul!" roared Mr. Banks. "You don't know what you're talking about. Dear old—my jumping godfathers, wait till you see her, that's all. Just wait till you see her!"

He seized his hat and waterproof.

"But, my dear!" cried Mrs. Banks, "you must be here to meet her. It looks so rude! Where are you going?"

"Anywhere. Everywhere. Tell her I'm dead!" he replied bitterly. And he hurried away from the house looking very nervous and depressed.

"My goodness, Michael, what *can* she be like?" said Jane.

"Curiosity killed the Cat," said Mary Poppins. "Put your hats on, please!"

She settled the Twins into the perambulator and pushed it down the garden path. Jane and Michael followed her out into the Lane.

"Where are we going to-day, Mary Poppins?"

"Across the Park and along the Thirty-Nine bus

route, up the High Street and over the Bridge and home through the Railway Arch!" she snapped.

"If we do that we'll be walking all night," whispered Michael, dropping behind with Jane. "And we'll miss Miss Andrew."

"She's going to stay for a month," Jane reminded him.

"But I want to see her arrive," he complained, dragging his feet and shuffling along the pavement.

"Step along, please," said Mary Poppins, briskly. "I might as well be taking a stroll with a couple of snails as you two!"

But when they caught up with her she kept them waiting for quite five minutes outside a fried-fish shop while she looked at herself in the window.

She was wearing her new white blouse with the pink spots and her face, as she beheld herself reflected

back from the piles of fried whiting, had a pleased
and satisfied air. She pushed back her coat a little so
that more of the blouse was visible and she thought
that, on the whole, she had never seen Mary Poppins
look nicer. Even the fried fish, with their fried tails
curled into their mouths, seemed to gaze at her with
round admiring eyes.

Mary Poppins gave a little conceited nod to her
reflection and hurried on. They had passed the High
Street now and were crossing the Bridge. Soon they
came to the Railway Arch and Jane and Michael
sprang eagerly ahead of the perambulator and ran all
the way until they turned the corner of Cherry Tree
Lane.

"There's a cab," cried Michael excitedly. "That
must be Miss Andrew's."

They stood still at the corner waiting for Mary
Poppins and watching for Miss Andrew.

A Taxi-cab, moving slowly down the Lane, drew
up at the gate of Number Seventeen. It groaned and
rattled as the engine stopped. And this was not sur-
prising for from wheel to roof it was heavily weighted
with luggage. You could hardly see the cab itself for
the trunks on the roof and the trunks at the back and
the trunks on either side.

Suit-cases and hampers could be seen half in and
half out of the windows. Hat-boxes were strapped to
the steps and two large Gladstone bags appeared to
be sitting in the Driver's seat.

Presently the Driver himself emerged from under
them. He climbed out carefully as though he were
descending a steep mountain, and opened the door.

A boot-box came bounding out, followed by a large
brown-paper parcel and after these came an umbrella
and a walking-stick tied together with string. Last of
all a small weighing-machine clattered down from the
rack, knocking the Taxi-man down.

"Be careful! Be careful!" a huge, trumpeting voice
shouted from inside the Taxi. "This is valuable
luggage!"

"And I'm a valuable driver!" retorted the Taxi-
man, picking himself up and rubbing his ankle.
"You seem to 'ave forgotten that, 'aven't you?"

"Make way, please, make way! I'm coming out!"
called the huge voice again.

And at that moment there appeared on the step of
the cab the largest foot the children had ever seen.
It was followed by the rest of Miss Andrew.

A large coat with a fur collar was wrapped about
her, a man's felt hat was perched on her head and
from the hat floated a long grey veil.

The children crept cautiously along by the fence,
gazing with interest at the huge figure, with its beaked
nose, grim mouth and small eyes that peered angrily
from behind glasses. They were almost deafened by
her voice as she argued with the Taxi-man.

"Four and threepence!" she was saying. "Prepos-
terous! I could go half-way round the world for that
amount. I shan't pay it! And I shall report you to the
Police."

The Taxi-man shrugged his shoulders. "That's the
fare," he said calmly. "If you can read, you can read
it on the meter. You can't go driving in a Taxi for
love you know, not with this luggage."

Miss Andrew snorted and, diving her hand into her large pocket took out a very small purse. She handed over a coin. The Taxi-man looked at it, turned it over and over in his hand as if he thought it a curiosity. Then he laughed rudely.

"This for the Driver?" he remarked sarcastically.

"Certainly not. It's your fare. I don't approve of tips," said Miss Andrew.

"You wouldn't," said the Taxi-man, staring at her.

And to himself he remarked—"Enough luggage to fill 'arf the Park and she doesn't approve of tips— the 'Arpy!"

But Miss Andrew did not hear him. The children had arrived at the gate and she turned to greet them, her feet ringing on the pavement and the veil flowing out behind her.

"Well?" she said gruffly, smiling a thin smile. "I don't suppose you know who *I* am?"

"Oh, yes we do!" said Michael. He spoke in his friendliest voice for he was very glad to meet Miss Andrew. "You're the Holy Terror!"

A dark purple flush rose up from Miss Andrew's neck and flooded her face.

"You are a very rude, impertinent boy. I shall report you to your Father!"

Michael looked surprised. "I didn't mean to be rude," he began. "It was Daddy who said——"

"Tut! Silence! Don't dare to argue with me!" said Miss Andrew. She turned to Jane.

"And you're Jane, I suppose? H'm. I never cared for the name."

"How do you do?" said Jane, politely, but secretly

thinking she did not care much for the name Euphemia.

"That dress is much too short!" trumpeted Miss
Andrew, "and you ought to be wearing stockings.
Little girls in my day never had bare legs. I shall
speak to your Mother."

"I don't like stockings," said Jane. "I only wear
them in the Winter."

"Don't be impudent. Children should be seen and
not heard!" said Miss Andrew.

She leant over the perambulator and with her huge
hand, pinched the Twin's cheeks in greeting.

John and Barbara began to cry.

"Tut! What manners!" exclaimed Miss Andrew.
"Brimstone and treacle—that's what they need!" she
went on, turning to Mary Poppins. "No well-brought-
up child cries like that. Brimstone and treacle. And
plenty of it. Don't forget!"

"Thank you, ma'am," said Mary Poppins with icy
politeness. "But I bring the children up in my own
way and take advice from nobody."

Miss Andrew stared. She looked as if she could not
believe her ears.

Mary Poppins stared back, calm and unafraid.

"Young woman!" said Miss Andrew, drawing herself up. "You forget yourself. How dare you answer
me like that! I shall take steps to have you removed
from this establishment! Mark my words!"

She flung open the gate and strode up the path,
furiously swinging the circular object under the
checked cloth, and saying "Tut-tut!" over and over
again.

Mrs. Banks came running out to meet her.

"Welcome, Miss Andrew, welcome!" she said politely. "How kind of you to pay us a visit. Such an unexpected pleasure. I hope you had a good journey."

"Most unpleasant. I never enjoy travelling," said Miss Andrew. She glanced with an angry, peering eye round the garden.

"Disgracefully untidy!" she remarked disgustedly. "Take my advice and dig up those things——" she pointed to the sun-flowers, "and plant evergreens. Much less trouble. Saves time *and* money. And looks neater. Better still, no garden at all. Just a plain cement courtyard."

"But," protested Mrs. Banks gently, "I like flowers best!"

"Ridiculous! Stuff and nonsense! You are a silly woman. And your children are very rude—especially the boy."

"Oh, Michael—I *am* surprised! Were you rude to Miss Andrew? You must apologise at once." Mrs. Banks was getting very nervous and flustered.

"No, Mother, I wasn't. I only——" He began to explain but Miss Andrew's loud voice interrupted.

"He was most insulting," she insisted. "He must go to a boarding-school at once. And the girl must have a Governess. I shall choose one myself. And as for the young person you have looking after them——" she nodded in the direction of Mary Poppins, "you must dismiss her this instant. She is impertinent, incapable and totally unreliable."

Mrs. Banks was plainly horrified.

"Oh, surely you are mistaken, Miss Andrew! We think she is such a treasure."

"You know nothing about it. I am *never* mistaken. Dismiss her!"

Miss Andrew swept on up the path.

Mrs. Banks hurried behind her looking very worried and upset.

"I—er—hope we shall be able to make you comfortable, Miss Andrew!" she said, politely. But she was beginning to feel rather doubtful.

"H'm. It's not much of a house," replied Miss
Andrew. "And it's in a shocking condition—peeling
everywhere and most dilapidated. You must send for
a carpenter. And when were these steps white-washed?
They're very dirty."

Mrs. Banks bit her lip. Miss Andrew was turning
her lovely, comfortable house into something mean
and shabby and it made her feel very unhappy.

"I'll have them done to-morrow," she said meekly.

"Why not to-day?" demanded Miss Andrew. "No
time like the present. And why paint your door
white? Dark brown—that's the proper colour for a
door. Cheaper, and doesn't show the dirt. Just look
at those spots!"

And putting down the circular object, she began
to point out the marks on the front door.

"There! There! There! Everywhere! Most disrepu-
table!"

"I'll see to it immediately," said Mrs. Banks faintly.
"Won't you come upstairs now to your room?"

Miss Andrew stamped into the hall after her.

"I hope there is a fire in it."

"Oh, yes. A good one. This way, Miss Andrew.
Robertson Ay will bring up your luggage."

"Well, tell him to be careful. The trunks are full
of medicine bottles. I have to take care of my health!"
Miss Andrew moved towards the stairs. She glanced
round the hall.

"This wall needs re-papering. I shall speak to
George about it. And why, I should like to know,
wasn't he here to meet me? Very rude of him. His
manners, I see, have not improved!"

The voice grew a little fainter as Miss Andrew followed Mrs. Banks upstairs. Far away the children could hear their Mother's gentle voice, meekly agreeing to do whatever Miss Andrew wished.

Michael turned to Jane.

"Who is George?" he asked.

"Daddy."

"But his name is Mr. Banks."

"Yes, but his other name is George."

Michael siged.

"A month is an awfully long time, Jane, isn't it?"

"Yes—four weeks and a bit," said Jane, feeling that a month with Miss Andrew would seem more like a year.

Michael edged closer to her.

"I say——" he began in an anxious whisper. "She can't really make them send Mary Poppins away, can she?"

"No, I don't think so. But she's very odd. I don't wonder Daddy went out."

"Odd!"

The word sounded behind them like an explosion.

They turned. Mary Poppins was gazing after Miss Andrew with a look that could have killed her.

"Odd!" she repeated with a long-drawn sniff. "*That's* not the word for her. Humph! I don't know how to bring up children, don't I? I'm impertinent, incapable, and totally unreliable, am I? We'll see about that!"

Jane and Michael were used to threats from Mary Poppins but to-day there was a note in her voice they had never heard before. They stared at her in silence, wondering what was going to happen.

A tiny sound, partly a sigh and partly a whistle, fell on the air.

"What was that?" said Jane quickly.

The sound came again, a little louder this time. Mary Poppins cocked her head and listened.

Again a faint chirping seemed to come from the doorstep.

"Ah!" cried Mary Poppins, triumphantly. "I might have known it!"

And with a sudden movement, she sprang at the circular object Miss Andrew had left behind and tweaked off the cover.

Beneath it was a brass bird-cage, very neat and shiny. And sitting at one end of the perch, huddled between his wings, was a small light-brown bird. He blinked a little as the afternoon light streamed down upon his head. Then he gazed solemnly about him with a round dark eye. His glance fell upon Mary Poppins and with a start of recognition he opened his beak and gave a sad, throaty little cheep. Jane and Michael had never heard such a miserable sound.

"Did she, indeed? Tch, tch, tch! You don't say!" said Mary Poppins nodding her head sympathetically.

"Chirp-irrup!" said the bird, shrugging its wings dejectedly.

"What? Two years? In that cage? Shame on her!" said Mary Poppins to the bird, her face flushing with anger.

The children stared. The bird was speaking in no language they knew and yet here was Mary Poppins carrying on an intelligent conversation with him as though she understood.

"What is it saying——" Michael began.

"Sh!" said Jane, pinching his arm to make him keep quiet.

They stared at the bird in silence. Presently he hopped a little way along the perch towards Mary Poppins and sang a note or two in a low questioning voice.

Mary Poppins nodded. "Yes—of course I know that field. Was that where she caught you?"

The bird nodded. Then he sang a quick trilling phrase that sounded like a question.

Mary Poppins thought for a moment. "Well," she said. "It's not very far. You could do it in about an hour. Flying South from here."

The bird seemed pleased. He danced a little on his perch and flapped his wings excitedly. Then his song broke out again, a stream of round, clear notes, as he looked imploringly at Mary Poppins.

She turned her head and glanced cautiously up the stairs.

"*Will* I? What do *you* think? Didn't you hear her call me a Young Person? Me!" She sniffed disgustedly.

The bird's shoulders shook as though he were laughing.

Mary Poppins bent down.

"What are you going to do, Mary Poppins?" cried Michael, unable to contain himself any longer. "What kind of a bird is that?"

"A lark," said Mary Poppins, briefly, turning the

handle of the little door. "You're seeing a lark in a cage for the first time—and the last!"

And as she said that the door of the cage swung open. The Lark, flapping his wings, swooped out with a shrill cry and alighted on Mary Poppins' shoulder.

"Humph!" she said, turning her head. "That's an improvement, I should think?"

"Chirr-up!" agreed the Lark, nodding.

"Well, you'd better be off," Mary Poppins warned him. "She'll be back in a minute."

At that the Lark burst into a stream of running notes, flicking its wings at her and bowing his head again and again.

"There, there!" said Mary Poppins, gruffly. "Don't thank me. I was glad to do it. I couldn't see a Lark in a cage! Besides, you heard what she called me!"

The Lark tossed back his head and fluttered his wings. He seemed to be laughing heartily. Then he cocked his head on one side and listened.

"Oh, I quite forgot!" came a trumpeting voice from upstairs. "I left Caruso outside. On those dirty steps. I must go and get him."

Miss Andrew's heavy tread sounded on the stairs.

"What?" she called back in reply to some question of Mrs. Banks. "Oh, he's my lark, my lark, Caruso! I call him that because he used to be such a beautiful singer. What? No, he doesn't sing at all now, not since I trapped him in the field and put him in a cage. I can't think why."

The voice was coming nearer, growing louder as it approached.

"Certainly not!" it called back to Mrs. Banks. "I will fetch him myself. I wouldn't trust one of those impudent children with him. Your banisters want polishing. They should be done at once."

Tramp-tramp. Tramp-tramp. Miss Andrew's steps sounded through the hall.

"Here she comes!" hissed Mary Poppins. "Be off with you!" She gave her shoulder a little shake.

"Quickly!" cried Michael anxiously.

"Oh, hurry!" said Jane.

The Twins waved their hands.

With a quick movement the Lark bent his head and pulled out one of his wing feathers with his beak.

"Chirr-chirr-chirr-irrup!" he sang and stuck the feather into the ribbon of Mary Poppins' hat. Then he spread his wings and swept into the air.

At the same moment Miss Andrew appeared in the doorway.

"What?" she shouted, when she saw Jane and Michael and the Twins. "Not gone up to bed yet? This will never do. All well-brought-up children——" she looked balefully at Mary Poppins, "should be in bed by five o'clock. I shall certainly speak to your Father."

She glanced round.

"Now, let me see. Where did I leave my——" She broke off suddenly. The uncovered cage, with its open door, stood at her feet. She stared down at it as though she were unable to believe her eyes.

"Why? When? Where? What? Who?" she spluttered. Then she found her full voice.

"Who took off that cover?" she thundered. The children trembled at the sound.

"Who opened that cage?"

There was no reply.

"Where is my Lark?"

Still there was silence as Miss Andrew stared from one child to another. At last her gaze fell accusingly upon Mary Poppins.

"You did it!" she cried, pointing her large finger. "I can tell by the look on your face! How dare you! I shall see that you leave this house to-night—bag and baggage! You impudent, impertinent, worthless——"

Chirp-irrup!

From the air came a little trill of laughter. Miss Andrew looked up. The Lark was lightly balancing on his wings just above the sunflowers.

"Ah, Caruso—there you are!" cried Miss Andrew. "Now come along! Don't keep me waiting. Come back to your nice, clean cage, Caruso, and let me shut the door!"

But the Lark just hung in the air and went into peals of laughter, flinging back his head and clapping his wings against his sides.

Miss Andrew bent and picked up the cage and held it above her head.

"Caruso—what did I say? Come back at once!" she commanded, swinging the cage towards him. But he swooped past it and brushed against Mary Poppins' hat.

"Chirp-irrup!" he said, as he sped by.

"All right," said Mary Poppins, nodding in reply.

"Caruso, did you hear me?" cried Miss Andrew.

But now there was a hint of dismay in her loud voice. She put down the cage and tried to catch the Lark with her hands. But he dodged and flickered past her, and with a lift of his wings, dived higher into the air.

A babble of notes streamed down to Mary Poppins.

"Ready!" she called back.

And then a strange thing happened.

Mary Poppins fixed her eyes upon Miss Andrew and Miss Andrew, suddenly spell-bound by that strange dark gaze, began to tremble on her feet. She gave a little gasp, staggered uncertainly forward and with a thundering rush she dashed towards the cage. Then—was it that Miss Andrew grew smaller or the cage larger? Jane and Michael could not be sure. All they knew for certain was that the cage door shut to with a little click and closed upon Miss Andrew.

"Oh! Oh! Oh!" she cried, as the Lark swooped down and seized the cage by the handle.

"What am I doing? Where am I going?" Miss Andrew shouted as the cage swept into the air.

"I have no room to move! I can hardly breathe!" she cried.

"Neither could he!" said Mary Poppins quietly.

Miss Andrew rattled at the bars of the cage.

"Open the door! Open the door! Let me out, I say! Let me out!"

"Humph! Not likely," said Mary Poppins in a low, scoffing voice.

On and on went the Lark, climbing higher and higher and singing as he went. And the heavy cage,

"Let me out! Let me out, I say!"

with Miss Andrew inside it, lurched after him, swaying dangerously as it swung from his claw.

Above the clear song of the Lark they heard Miss
Andrew hammering at the bars and crying:

"I who was Well-Brought-Up! I who was Always
Right! I who was Never Mistaken. That I should
come to this!"

Mary Poppins gave a curious, quiet little laugh.

The Lark looked very small now, but still he
circled upwards, singing loudly and triumphantly.
And still Miss Andrew and her cage circled heavily
after him, rocking from side to side, like a ship in
a storm.

"Let me out, I say! Let me out!" Her voice came
screaming down.

Suddenly the Lark changed his direction. His song
ceased for a moment as he darted sideways. Then it
began again, wild and clear, as shaking the ring of
the cage from his foot, he flew towards the South.

"He's off!" said Mary Poppins.

"Where?" cried Jane and Michael.

"Home—to his meadows," she replied, gazing upwards.

"But he's dropped the cage!" said Michael, staring.

And well he might stare, for the cage was now
hurtling downwards, lurching and tumbling, end
over end. They could clearly see Miss Andrew, now
standing on her head and now on her feet as the
cage turned through the air. Down, down, it came,
heavy as a stone, and landed with a plop on the top
step.

With a fierce movement, Miss Andrew tore open

the door. And it seemed to Jane and Michael as she came out that she was as large as ever and even more frightful.

For a moment she stood there, panting, unable to speak, her face purplier than before.

"How dare you!" she said in a throaty whisper, pointing a trembling finger at Mary Poppins. And Jane and Michael saw that her eyes were no longer angry and scornful, but full of terror.

"You—you——" stammered Miss Andrew huskily, "you cruel, disrespectful, unkind, wicked, wilful girl —how could you, how could you?"

Mary Poppins fixed her with a look. From half-closed eyes, she gazed revengefully at Miss Andrew for a long moment.

"You said I didn't know how to bring up children," she said, speaking slowly and distinctly.

Miss Andrew shrank back, trembling with fear.

"I—I apologise," she said, gulping.

"That I was impudent, incapable, and totally unreliable," said the quiet, implacable voice.

Miss Andrew cowered beneath the steady gaze.

"It was a mistake. I—I'm sorry," she stammered.

"That I was a Young Person!" continued Mary Poppins, remorselessly.

"I take it back," panted Miss Andrew. "All of it. Only let me go. I ask nothing more." She clasped her hands and gazed at Mary Poppins, imploringly.

"I can't stay here," she whispered. "No, no! Not here! I beg you to let me go!"

Mary Poppins gazed at her, long and thoughtfully. Then with a little outward movement of her hand, "Go!" she said.

Miss Andrew gave a gasp of relief. "Oh, thank you! Thank you!" Still keeping her eyes fixed on Mary Poppins she staggered backwards down the steps, then she turned and went stumbling unevenly down the garden path.

The Taxi-man, who all this time had been unloading the luggage, was starting up his engine and preparing to depart.

Miss Andrew held up a trembling hand.

"Wait!" she cried brokenly. "Wait for me. You shall have a ten shilling note for yourself if you will drive me away at once."

The man stared at her.

"I mean it!" she said urgently. "See," she fumbled feverishly in her pocket, "here it is. Take it—and drive on!"

Miss Andrew tottered into the cab and collapsed upon the seat.

The Taxi-man, still gaping, closed the door upon her.

Then he began hurriedly re-loading the luggage. Robertson Ay had fallen asleep across a pile of trunks, but the Taxi-man did not stop to wake him. He swept him off on to the path and finished the work himself.

"Looks as though the 'ole girl 'ad 'ad a shock! I never saw anybody take on so. Never!" he murmured to himself as he drove off.

But what kind of a shock it was the Taxi-man did not know and, if he lived to be a hundred, could not possibly guess. . . .

"Where is Miss Andrew?" said Mrs. Banks, hurrying to the front door in search of the visitor.

"Gone," said Michael.

"What do you mean—gone?" Mrs. Banks looked very surprised.

"She didn't seem to want to stay," said Jane.

Mrs. Banks frowned.

"What does this mean, Mary Poppins?" she demanded.

"I couldn't say, m'm, I'm sure," said Mary Poppins, calmly, as though the matter did not interest her. She glanced down at her new blouse and smoothed out a crease.

Mrs. Banks looked from one to the other and shook her head.

"How very extraordinary! I can't understand it."

Just then the garden gate opened and shut with a quiet little click. Mr. Banks came tip-toeing up the path. He hesitated and waited nervously on one foot as they all turned towards him.

"Well? Has she come?" he said anxiously, in a loud whisper.

"She has come and gone," said Mrs. Banks.

Mr. Banks stared.

"Gone? Do you mean—really gone? Miss Andrew?"

Mrs. Banks nodded.

"Oh, joy, joy!" cried Mr. Banks, and seizing the skirts of his waterproof in both hands he proceeded to dance the Highland Fling in the middle of the path. He stopped suddenly.

"But how? When? Why?" he asked.

"Just now—in a taxi. Because the children were rude to her, I suppose. She complained to me about them. I simply can't think of any other reason. Can you, Mary Poppins?"

"No, m'm, I can't," said Mary Poppins, brushing a speck of dust off her blouse with great care.

Mr. Banks turned to Jane and Michael with a sorrowful look on his face.

"You were rude to Miss Andrew? My Governess? That dear old soul? I'm ashamed of you both—thoroughly ashamed." He spoke sternly, but there was a laughing twinkle in his eyes.

"I'm a most unfortunate man," he went on, putting his hands into his pockets. "Here am I slaving day in and day out to bring you up properly, and how do you repay me? By being rude to Miss Andrew! It's shameful! It's outrageous. I don't know that I shall ever be able to forgive you. But——" he continued, taking two sixpences out of his pocket and solemnly offering one to each of them, "I shall do my best to forget!"

He turned away smiling.

"Hullo!" he remarked, stumbling against the birdcage. "Where did this come from? Whose is it?"

Jane and Michael and Mary Poppins were silent.

"Well, never mind," said Mr. Banks. "It's mine now. I shall keep it in the garden and train my sweet-peas over it."

And he went off, carrying the bird-cage and whistling very happily. . . .

"Well," said Mary Poppins, sternly, as she followed them into the Nursery. "This is nice goings on, I must say. You behaving so rudely to your Father's guest."

"But we weren't rude," Michael protested. "I only said she was a Holy Terror and he called her that himself."

"Sending her away like that when she'd only just come—don't you call that rude?" demanded Mary Poppins.

"But we didn't," said Jane. "It was you——"

"*I* was rude to your father's guest?" Mary Poppins, with her hands on her hips, eyed Jane furiously. "Do you dare to stand there and tell me that?"

"No, no! You weren't rude, but——"

"I should think not, indeed," retorted Mary Poppins, taking off her hat and unfolding her apron. "*I* was properly brought up!" she added sniffing, as she began to undress the Twins.

Michael sighed. He knew it was no use arguing with Mary Poppins.

He glanced at Jane. She was turning her sixpence over and over in her hand.

"Michael!" she said. "I've been thinking."

"What?"

"Daddy gave us these because he thought *we* sent Miss Andrew away."

"I know."

"And we didn't. It was Mary Poppins!"

Michael shuffled his feet.

"Then you think——" he began uneasily, hoping she didn't mean what he thought she meant.

"Yes, I do," said Jane nodding.

"But—but I wanted to spend mine."

"So did I. But it wouldn't be fair. They're hers really."

Michael thought about it for a long time. Then he sighed.

"All right," he said regretfully and took his sixpence out of his pocket.

They went together to Mary Poppins.

Jane held out the coins.

"Here you are!" she said, breathlessly, "we think you should have them."

Mary Poppins took the sixpences and turned them over and over on her palm—heads first and then tails. Then her eye caught theirs and it seemed to them that her look plunged right down inside them and *saw* what they were thinking. For a long time she stood there, staring down into their thoughts.

"Humph!" she said at last, slipping the sixpences into her apron pocket. "Take care of the pennies and the pounds will take care of themselves."

"I expect you'll find them very useful," said Michael, gazing sadly at the pocket.

"I expect I shall," she retorted tartly, as she went to turn on the bath. . . .

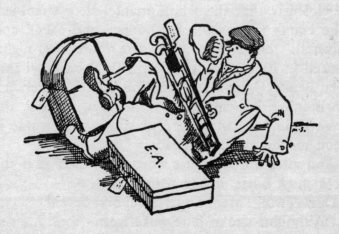

CHAPTER

3

BAD WEDNESDAY

TICK-TACK! Tick-tock!

The pendulum of the Nursery clock swung backwards and forwards like an old lady nodding her head.

Tick-tack! Tick-tock!

Then the clock stopped ticking and began to whir and growl, quietly at first and then more loudly, as though it were in pain. And as it whirred it shook so violently that the whole mantel-piece trembled. The empty marmalade jar hopped and shook and shivered; John's hair-brush, left there over-night, danced in its bristles; the Royal Doulton Bowl that Mrs. Banks' Great-Aunt Caroline had given her as a Christening Present slipped sideways, so that the three little boys who were playing horses inside it stood on their painted heads.

And after all that, just when it seemed as if the clock must burst, it began to strike.

One! Two! Three! Four! Five! Six! Seven!

On the last stroke Jane woke up.

The sun was streaming in through a gap in the curtains and falling in gold stripes upon her quilt. Jane sat up and looked round the Nursery. No sound

54

came from Michael's bed. The Twins in their cots
were sucking their thumbs and breathing deeply.

"I'm the only one awake," she said, feeling very
pleased. "Everybody in the world is asleep except

me. I can lie here all by myself and think and think
and think."

And she drew her knees up to her chin and curled
into the bed as though she were settling down into a
nest.

"Now I am a bird!" she said to herself. "I have just.

laid seven lovely white eggs and I am sitting with my wings over them, brooding. Cluck-cluck! Cluck-cluck!"

She made a small broody noise in her throat.

"And after a long time, say half an hour, there will be a little cheep, and a little tap and the shells will crack. Then, out will pop seven little chicks, three yellow, two brown and two——"

"Time to get up!"

Mary Poppins, appearing suddenly from nowhere, tweaked the bed-clothes from Jane's shoulders.

"Oh, no, NO!" grumbled Jane, pulling them up again.

She felt very cross with Mary Poppins for rushing in and spoiling everything.

"I don't want to get up!" she said, turning her face into the pillow.

"Oh, indeed?" Mary Poppins said calmly, as though the remark had no interest for her. She pulled the bed-clothes right off the bed and Jane found herself standing on the floor.

"Oh, dear," she grumbled, "why do I always have to get up first?"

"You're the eldest—that's why." Mary Poppins pushed her towards the bath-room.

"But I don't *want* to be the eldest. Why can't Michael be the eldest sometimes?"

"Because you were born first—see?"

"Well, I didn't ask to be. I'm tired of being born first. I wanted to think."

"You can think when you're brushing your teeth."

"Not the same thoughts."

"Well, nobody wants to think the same thoughts all the time!"

"I do."

Mary Poppins gave her a quick, black look.

"That's enough, thank you!" And from the tone in her voice Jane knew she meant what she said.

Mary Poppins hurried away to wake Michael.

Jane put down her toothbrush and sat on the edge of the bath.

"It's not fair," she grumbled, kicking the linoleum with her toes. "Making me do all the horrid things just because I'm the eldest! I won't brush my teeth!"

Immediately she felt surprised at herself. She was usually quite glad to be older than Michael and the Twins. It made her feel rather superior and much more important. But to-day—what was the matter with to-day that she felt so cross and peevish?

"If Michael had been born first I'd have had time to hatch out my eggs!" She grumbled to herself, feeling that the day had begun badly.

Unfortunately, instead of getting better, it grew worse.

At breakfast Mary Poppins discovered there was only enough Puffed Rice for three.

"Well, Jane must have Porridge," she said, setting out the plates and sniffing angrily for she did not like making Porridge. There were always too many lumps in it.

"But why?" complained Jane. "I want Puffed Rice."

Mary Poppins darted a fierce look at her.

"Because you're the eldest!"

There it was again! That hateful word. She kicked the leg of her chair under the table, hoping she was scratching off the varnish, and ate her porridge as slowly as she dared. She turned it round and round in her mouth swallowing as little as possible. It would serve everybody right if she starved to death. Then they'd be sorry!

"What is to-day?" enquired Michael cheerfully, scraping up the last of his Puffed Rice.

"Wednesday," said Mary Poppins. "Leave the pattern on the plate, please!"

"Then it's to-day we're going to tea with Miss Lark!"

"*If* you're good," said Mary Poppins darkly, as though she did not believe such a thing was possible.

But Michael was in a cheerful mood and took no notice.

"Wednesday!" he shouted, banging his spoon on the table. "That's the day Jane was born. Wednesday's child is full of woe. That's why she has to have porridge instead of rice," he said naughtily.

Jane frowned and kicked at him under the table. But he swung his legs aside and laughed.

"Monday's child is fair of face, Tuesday's child is full of grace!" He chanted. "That's true, too. The Twins are full of grace and they were born on a Tuesday. And I'm Monday—fair of face."

Jane laughed scornfully.

"I am," he insisted. "I heard Mrs. Brill say so. She told Ellen I was as handsome as half-a-crown."

"Well, that's not very handsome," said Jane. "Besides, your nose turns up."

Michael looked at her reproachfully. And again Jane felt surprised at herself. At any other time she would have agreed with him, for she thought Michael a very good-looking little boy. But now she said cruelly,

"Yes, and your toes turn in. Bandy-legs! Bandy-legs!"

Michael rushed at her.

"That will be enough from you!" said Mary Poppins, looking angrily at Jane. "And if any body in this house is a beauty it's——" She paused and glanced with a satisfied smile at her own reflection in the mirror.

"Who?" demanded Michael and Jane together.

"Nobody of the name of Banks!" retorted Mary Poppins. "So there!"

Michael looked across at Jane as he always did when Mary Poppins made one of her curious remarks. But though she felt his look she pretended not to notice. She turned away and took her paint-box from the toy-cupboard.

"Won't you play trains?" asked Michael, trying to be friendly.

"No, I won't. I want to be by myself."

"Well, darlings, and how are you all this morning?"

Mrs. Banks came running into the room and kissed them hurriedly. She was always so busy that she never had time to walk.

"Michael," she said, "you must have some new slippers—your toes are coming out at the top. Mary Poppins, John's curls will *have* to come off, I'm afraid. Barbara, my pet, don't suck your thumb! Jane, run downstairs and ask Mrs. Brill not to ice the plum cake, I want a plain one."

There they were again, breaking into her day! As soon as she began to do anything they made her stop and do something else.

"Oh, Mother, must I? Why can't Michael?"

Mrs. Banks looked surprised.

"But I thought you liked helping! And Michael always forgets the message. Besides, you're the eldest. Run along."

She went downstairs as slowly as she could. She hoped she would be so late with the message that Mrs. Brill would have already iced the cake.

And all the time she felt astonished at the way she was behaving. It was as if there was another person inside her—somebody with a very bad temper and an ugly face—who was making her feel cross.

She gave the message to Mrs. Brill and was disappointed to find that she was in plenty of time.

"Well, that'll save a penn'orth of trouble anyway." Mrs. Brill remarked.

"And, Dearie," she went on, "you might just slip out into the garden and tell that Robertson he hasn't done the knives. My legs are bad and they're my only pair."

"I can't. I'm busy."

It was Mrs. Brill's turn to look surprised.

"Ah, be a kind girl, then—it's all I can do to stand, let alone walk!"

Jane sighed. Why couldn't they leave her alone?

She kicked the kitchen door shut and dawdled out into the garden.

Robertson Ay was asleep on the path with his head on the watering-can. His lank hair rose and fell as he snored. It was Robertson Ay's special gift that he could sleep anywhere and at any time. In fact, he preferred sleeping to waking. And, usually, whenever they could, Jane and Michael prevented him from being found out. But to-day was different. The bad-tempered person inside her didn't care a bit what happened to Robertson Ay.

"I hate everybody!" she said, and rapped sharply on the watering-can.

Robertson Ay sat up with a start.

"Help! Murder! Fire!" he cried, waving his arms wildly.

Then he rubbed his eyes and saw Jane.

"Oh, it's only you!" he said, in a disappointed voice as if he had hoped for something more exciting.

"You're to go and do the knives at once," she ordered.

Robertson Ay got slowly to his feet and shook himself.

"Ah," he said sadly, "it's always something. If it's not one thing, it's another. I ought to be resting. I never get a moment's peace."

"Yes, you do!" said Jane cruelly. "You get nothing but peace. You're always asleep."

A hurt, reproachful look came over Robertson Ay's face and at any other time it would have made her feel ashamed. But to-day she wasn't a bit sorry.

"Saying such things!" said Robertson Ay sadly.

"And you the eldest and all. I wouldn't have thought it—not if I'd done nothing but think for the rest of my life."

And he gave her a sorrowful glance and shuffled slowly away to the kitchen.

She wondered if he would ever forgive her. And, as if in reply, the sulky creature inside her said, "I don't care if he doesn't!"

She tossed her head and went slowly back to the Nursery dragging her sticky hands along the fresh white wall because she had always been told not to.

Mary Poppins was flicking her feather duster round the furniture.

"Off to a funeral?" she enquired as Jane appeared.

Jane looked sulky and did not answer.

"I know somebody who's looking for Trouble. And he that seeks shall find!"

"I don't care!"

"Don't Care was made care! Don't Care was hung!" jeered Mary Poppins, putting the duster away.

"And now——" she looked warningly at Jane. "I am going to have my dinner. You are to look after the little ones and if I hear One Word——" She did not finish the sentence but she gave a long threatening sniff as she went out of the room.

John and Barbara ran to Jane and caught her hands. But she uncurled their fingers and crossly pushed them away.

"I wish I were an only child," she said bitterly.

"Why don't you run away," suggested Michael. "Somebody might adopt you."

Jane looked up, startled and surprised.

"But you'd miss me!"

"No, I wouldn't," he said stoutly. "Not if you're always going to be cross. Besides, then I could have your paint-box."

"No, you couldn't," she said jealously. "I'd take it with me."

And, just to show him that the paint-box was hers and not his, she got out the brushes and the painting-book and spread them on the floor.

"Paint the clock," said Michael helpfully.

"No."

"Well, the Royal Doulton Bowl."

Jane glanced up. The three little boys were racing over the field inside the green rim of the bowl. At any other time she would have liked to paint them but to-day she was not going to be pleasant or obliging.

"I won't. I will paint what *I* want."

And she began to make a picture of herself, quite alone, brooding over her eggs.

Michael and John and Barbara sat on the floor watching.

Jane was so

interested in her eggs that she almost forgot her bad temper.

Michael leaned forward. "Why not put in a hen—just there!"

He pointed to a spare white patch, brushing against John with his arm. Over went John, falling sideways and upsetting the cup with his foot. The coloured water splashed out and flooded the picture.

With a cry Jane sprang to her feet.

"Oh, I can't bear it. You great Clumsy! You've spoilt everything!"

And, rushing at Michael, she punched him so violently that he, too, toppled over and crashed down on top of John. A squeal of pain and terror broke from the Twins, and above their cries rose Michael's voice wailing "My head is broken! What shall I do? My head is broken!" over and over again.

"I don't care, I don't care!" shouted Jane. "You wouldn't leave me alone and you've spoilt my picture. I hate you, I hate you, I hate——!"

The door burst open.

Mary Poppins surveyed the scene with furious eyes.

"What did I say to you?" she enquired of Jane in a voice so quiet that it was terrible. "That if I heard One Word—and now look what I find! A nice party you'll have at Miss Lark's, I *don't* think! Not one step will you go out of this room this afternoon or I'm a Chinaman."

"I don't *want* to go. I'd rather stay here." Jane put her hands behind her back and sauntered away. She did not feel a bit sorry.

"Very good."

Mary Poppins voice was gentle but there was something very frightening in it.

Jane watched her dressing the others for the party. And when they were ready Mary Poppins took her best hat out of a brown-paper bag and set it on her head at a very smart angle. She clipped her gold locket round her neck and over it wound the red-and-white checked scarf Mrs. Banks had given her. At one end was stitched a white label marked with a large M.P., and Mary Poppins smiled at herself in the mirror as she tucked the label out of sight.

Then she took her parrot-handled umbrella from the cupboard, popped it under her arm and hurried the little ones down the stairs.

"Now you'll have time to think!" she remarked tartly and, with a loud sniff, shut the door behind her.

For a long time Jane sat staring in front of her. She tried to think about her seven eggs. But somehow they didn't interest her any more.

What were they doing now, at Miss Lark's? she wondered. Playing with Miss Lark's dogs, perhaps, and listening to Miss Lark telling them that Andrew had a wonderful pedigree but that Willoughby was half an Airdale and half a Retriever and the worst half of both. And presently they would all, even the dogs, have chocolate biscuits and walnut cake for tea.

"Oh, dear!"

The thought of all she was missing stirred angrily

inside Jane and when she remembered it was all her own fault she felt crosser than ever.

Tick-tack! Tick-tock! said the clock loudly.

"Oh, be quiet!" cried Jane furiously, and picking up her paint-box she hurled it across the room.

It crashed against the glass face of the clock and, glancing off, clattered down upon the Royal Doulton Bowl.

Crrrrrrack! The Bowl toppled sideways against the clock.

Oh! Oh! What had she done?

Jane shut her eyes, not daring to look and see.

"I say—that hurt!"

A clear reproachful voice sounded in the room.

Jane started and opened her eyes.

"Jane!" said the voice again. "That was my knee!"

She turned her head quickly. There was nobody in the room.

She ran to the door and opened it. Still nobody! Then somebody laughed.

"Here, silly!" said the voice again. "Up here!"

She looked up at the mantel-piece. Beside the clock lay the Royal Doulton Bowl with a large crack running right across it and, to her surprise, Jane saw that one of the painted boys had dropped the reins and was bending down holding his knee with both hands. The other two had turned and were looking at him sympathetically.

"But——" began Jane, half to herself and half to the unknown voice. "I don't understand." The boy in the Bowl lifted his head and smiled at her.

"Don't you? No, I suppose you don't. I've noticed

that you and Michael often don't understand the
simplest things—do they?"

He turned, laughing, to his brothers.

"No," said one of them, "not even how to keep
the Twins quiet!"

"Nor the proper way to draw bird's eggs—she's
made them all wriggly," said the other.

"How do you know about the Twins—and the
eggs?" said Jane, flushing.

"Gracious!" said the first boy. "You don't think
we could have watched you all this time without
knowing everything that happens in this room! We
can't see into the Night-nursery, of course, or the
bath-room. What coloured tiles has it?"

"Pink," said Jane.

"Ours has blue-and-white. Would you like to see
it?"

Jane hesitated. She hardly knew what to reply, she
was so astonished.

"Do come! William and Everard will be *your*
horses, if you like and I'll carry the whip and run
alongside. I'm Valentine, in case you don't know.
We're Triplets. And, of course, there Christina."

"Where's Christina?" Jane searched the Bowl. But
she saw only the green meadow and a little wood of
alders and Valentine, William and Everard standing
together.

"Come and see!" said Valentine persuasively, holding out his hand. "Why should the others have all
the fun? You come with us—into the Bowl!"

That decided her. She would show Michael that he
and the Twins were not the only ones who could go

to a party. She would make them jealous and sorry
for treating her so badly.

"All right," she said, putting out her hand. "I'll
come!"

Valentine's hand closed round her wrist and
pulled her towards the Bowl. And, suddenly, she was
no longer in the cool Day-Nursery but out in a wide
sunlit meadow, and instead of the ragged nursery
carpet, a springing turf of grass and daisies was
spread beneath her feet.

"Hooray!" said Valentine, William and Everard,
dancing round her. She noticed that Valentine was
limping.

"Oh," said Jane. "I forgot! Your knee!"

He smiled at her. "Never mind. It was the crack
that did it. I know you didn't mean to hurt me!"

Jane took out her handkerchief and bound it
round his knee.

"That's better!" he said politely, and put the reins
into her hand.

William and Everard, tossing their heads and
snorting, flew off across the meadow with Jane jingling the reins behind them.

Beside her, one foot heavy and one foot light, because of his knee, ran Valentine.

And as he ran, he sang—

> "My love, thou art a nosegay sweet,
>   My sweetest flower I prove thee;
> And pleased I pin thee to my breast,
>   And dearly I do love thee!"

William and Everard's voices came in with the chorus,

"And deeeee-arly I do lo-o-ove thee!"

Jane thought it was rather an old-fashioned song, but then, everything about the Triplets was old-fashioned—their long hair, their strange clothes and their polite way of speaking.

"It *is* odd!" she thought to herself, but she also thought that this was better than being at Miss Lark's, and that Michael would envy her when she told him all about it.

On ran the horses, tugging Jane after them, drawing her away and away from the Nursery.

Presently she pulled up, panting, and looked back over the tracks their feet had made in the grass. Behind her, at the other side of the meadow, she could see the outer rim of the Bowl. It seemed small and very far away. And something inside her warned her that it was time to turn back.

"I must go now," she said, dropping the jingling reins.

"Oh, no, no!" cried the Triplets, closing round her.

And now something in their voices made her feel uneasy.

"They'll miss me at home. I'm afraid I must go," she said quickly.

"It's quite early!" protested Valentine. "They'll still be at Miss Lark's. Come on. I'll show you my paint-box."

Jane was tempted.

"Has it got Chinese White?" she enquired. For Chinese White was just what her own paint-box lacked.

"Yes, in a silver tube. Come!"

Against her will Jane allowed him to draw her on-wards. She thought she would just have one look at the paint-box and then hurry back. She would not even ask to be allowed to use it.

"But where is your house? It isn't in the Bowl!"

"Of course it is! But you can't see it because it's behind the wood. Come on!"

They were drawing her now under dark alder boughs. The dead leaves cracked under their feet and every now and then a pigeon swooped from branch to branch with a loud clapping of wings. William showed Jane a robin's nest in a pile of twigs and Everard broke off a spray of leaves and twined it round her head. But in spite of their friendliness Jane was shy and nervous and she felt very glad when they reached the end of the wood.

"Here it is!" said Valentine, waving his hand.

And she saw rising before her a huge stone house covered with ivy. It was older than any house she had ever seen and it seemed to lean towards her threaten-ingly. On either side of the steps a stone lion crouched, as if waiting the moment to spring.

Jane shivered as the shadow of the house fell upon her.

"I can't stay long——" she said, uneasily. "It's get-ting late."

"Just five minutes!" pleaded Valentine, drawing her into the hall.

Their feet rang hollowly on the stone floor. There was no sign of any human being. Except for herself and the Triplets the house seemed deserted. A cold wind swept whistling along the corridor.

"Christina! Christina!" called Valentine, pulling Jane up the stairs. "Here she is!"

His cry went echoing round the house and every wall seemed to call back frighteningly,

"HERE SHE IS!"

There was a sound of running feet and a door burst open. A little girl, slightly taller than the Triplets and dressed in an old-fashioned, flowery dress, rushed out and flung herself upon Jane.

"At last, at last!" she cried triumphantly. "The boys have been watching for you for ages! But they couldn't catch you before—you were always so happy!"

"Catch me?" said Jane. "I don't understand!"

She was beginning to be frightened and to wish she had never come with Valentine into the Bowl.

"Great-Grandfather will explain," said Christina, laughing curiously. She drew Jane across the landing and through the door.

"Heh! Heh! Heh! What's this?" demanded a thin, cracked voice.

Jane stared and drew back against Christina. For at the far end of the room, on a seat by the fire, sat a figure that filled her with terror. The firelight flickered over a very old man, so old that he looked more like a shadow than a human being. From his thin mouth a thin grey beard straggled and, though he wore a smoking cap, Jane could see that he was as bald as an egg. He was dressed in a long old-fashioned dressing-gown of faded silk, and a pair of embroidered slippers hung on his thin feet.

"So!" said the shadowy figure, taking a long curved pipe from his mouth. "Jane has arrived at last."

He rose and came towards her smiling frighteningly, his eyes burning in their sockets with a bright steely fire.

"I hope you had a good journey, my dear!" he croaked. And drawing Jane to him with a bony hand he kissed her cheek. At the touch of his grey beard Jane started back with a cry.

"Heh! Heh! Heh!" He laughed his cackling, terrifying laugh.

"She came through the alder wood with the boys, Great-Grandfather," said Christina.

"Ah? How did they catch her?"

"She was cross at being the eldest. So she threw her paint-box at the Bowl and cracked Val's knee."

"So!" the horrible old voice whistled. "It was temper, was it? Well, well——" he laughed thinly, "now you'll be the youngest, my dear! My youngest Great-Grand-daughter. But I shan't allow any tempers here! Heh! Heh! Heh! Oh, dear, no. Well, come along and sit by the fire. Will you take tea or cherry-wine?"

"No, no!" Jane burst out. "I'm afraid there's been a mistake. I must go home now. I live at Number Seventeen Cherry Tree Lane."

"Used to, you mean," corrected Val triumphantly. "You live here now."

"But you don't understand!" Jane said desperately. "I don't want to live here. I want to go home."

"Do you think we will let you go?" he enquired

"Nonsense!" croaked the Great-Grandfather.
"Number Seventeen is a horrible place, mean and
stuffy and modern. Besides you're not happy there.
Heh! Heh! Heh! I know what it's like being the eld-
est—all the work and none of the fun. Heh! Heh!
But here——" he waved his pipe, "here you'll be the
Spoilt One, the Darling, the Treasure, and never go
back any more!"

"Never!" echoed William and Everard dancing
round her.

"Oh, I must. I will!" Jane cried, the tears springing
to her eyes.

The Great-Grandfather smiled his horrible tooth-
less smile.

"Do you think we will let you go?" he enquired,
his bright eyes burning. "You cracked our Bowl. You
must take the consequences. Christina, Valentine,
William and Everard want you for their youngest
sister. I want you for my youngest Great-Grandchild.
Besides, you owe us something. You hurt Valentine's
knee."

"I will make up to him. I will give him my paint-
box."

"He has one."

"My hoop."

"He has out-grown hoops."

"Well——" faltered Jane. "I will marry him when
I grow up."

The Great-Grandfather cackled with laughter.

Jane turned imploringly to Valentine. He shook
his head.

"I'm afraid it's too late for that," he said sadly. "I grew up long ago."

"Then why, then what—oh, I don't understand. Where am I?" cried Jane, gazing about her in terror.

"Far from home, my child, far from home," croaked the Great-Grandfather. "You are back in the Past— back where Christina and the boys were young sixty years ago!"

Through her tears Jane saw his old eyes burning fiercely.

"Then—how can I get home?" she whispered.

"You cannot. You will stay here. There is no other place for you. You are back in the Past, remember! The Twins and Michael, even your Father and Mother, are not yet born; Number Seventeen is not even built. You cannot go home!"

"No, no!" cried Jane. "It's not true! It can't be!" Her heart was thumping inside her. Never to see Michael again, nor the Twins, nor her Father and Mother and Mary Poppins!

And suddenly she began to shout, lifting her voice so that it echoed wildly through the stone corridors.

"Mary Poppins! I'm sorry I was cross! Oh, Mary Poppins, help me, help me!"

"Quick! Hold her close! Surround her!"

She heard the Great-Grandfather's sharp command. She felt the four children pressing close about her.

She shut her eyes tight. "Mary Poppins!" she cried again, "Mary Poppins!"

A hand caught hers and pulled her away from the circling arms of Christina, Valentine, William and Everard.

"Heh! Heh! Heh!"

The Great-Grandfather's cackling laugh echoed through the room. The grasp on her hand tightened and she felt herself being drawn away. She dared not look for fear of those frightening eyes but she pulled fiercely against the tugging hand.

"Heh! Heh! Heh!"

The laugh sounded again and the hand drew her on, down stone stairs and echoing corridors.

She had no hope now. Behind her the voices of Christina and the Triplets faded away. No help would come from them.

She stumbled desperately after the flying footsteps and felt, though her eyes were closed, dark shadows above her head and damp earth under her feet.

What was happening to her? Where, oh, where was she going? If only she hadn't been so cross—if only!

The strong hand pulled her onwards and presently she felt the warmth of sunlight on her cheeks and sharp grass scratched her legs as she was dragged along. Then suddenly a pair of arms, like bands of iron, closed about her, lifted her up and swung her through the air.

"Oh, help, help!" She cried, frantically twisting and turning against those arms. She would not give in without a struggle, she would kick and kick and kick and——

"I'll thank you to remember," said a familiar voice in her ear, "that this is my best skirt and it has to last me the Summer!"

Jane opened her eyes. A pair of fierce blue eyes looked steadily into hers.

The arms that folded her so closely were Mary Poppins' arms and the legs she was kicking so furiously were the legs of Mary Poppins.

"Oh!" she faltered. "It was *you*! I thought you hadn't heard me, Mary Poppins! I thought I should be kept there forever. I thought——"

"Some people," remarked Mary Poppins, putting her gently down, "think a great deal too much. Of that I'm sure. Wipe your face, please!"

She thrust her blue handkerchief into Jane's hand and began to get the Nursery ready for the evening.

Jane watched her, drying her tear-stained face on the large blue handkerchief. She glanced round the well-known room. There were the ragged carpet and the toy-cupboard and Mary Poppins' arm-chair. At

the sight of them she felt safe and warm and com-
forted. She listened to the familiar sounds as Mary
Poppins went about her work, and her terror died
away. A tide of happiness swept over her.

"It couldn't have been I who was cross!" she said
wonderingly to herself. "It must have been somebody
else."

Mary Poppins went to a drawer and took out the
Twins' clean nightgowns.

Jane ran to her.

"Shall I air them, Mary Poppins?"

Mary Poppins sniffed.

"Don't trouble, thank you. You're much too busy,
I'm sure! I'll get Michael to help me when he comes
up."

Jane blushed.

"Please let me," she said. "I like helping. Besides
I'm the eldest."

Mary Poppins put her hands on her hips and regarded Jane thoughtfully for a moment.

"Humph!" she said at last. "Don't burn them,
then! I've enough holes to mend as it is."

And she handed Jane the nightgowns.

"But it couldn't *really* have happened!" scoffed
Michael a little later when he heard of Jane's adventure. "You'd be much too big for the Bowl."

She thought for a moment. Somehow, as she told
the story, it did seem rather impossible.

"I suppose it couldn't," she admitted. "But it
seemed quite real at the time."

"I expect you just thought it. You're always thinking things." He felt rather superior because he himself didn't ever think at all.

"You two and your thoughts!" said Mary Poppins crossly, pushing them aside as she dumped the Twins into their cots.

"And now," she snapped, when John and Barbara were safely tucked in, "perhaps I shall have a moment to myself."

She took the pins out of her hat and thrust it back into its brown-paper bag. She unclipped the locket and put it carefully away in a drawer. Then she slipped off her coat, shook it out, and hung it on the peg behind the door.

"Why, where's your new scarf?" said Jane. "Have you lost it?"

"She couldn't have," said Michael. "She had it on when she came home. I saw it."

Mary Poppins turned on them.

"Be good enough to mind your own affairs," she said snappily, "and let me mind mine!"

"I only wanted to help——" Jane began.

"I can help myself, thank you!" said Mary Poppins, sniffing.

Jane turned to exchange looks with Michael. But this time it was he who took no notice. He was staring at the mantel-piece as if he could not believe his eyes.

"What is it, Michael?"

"You didn't just think it, after all!" he whispered, pointing.

Jane looked up at the mantel-piece. There lay the Royal Doulton Bowl with the crack running right

across it. There were the meadow grasses and the
wood of alders. And there were the three little boys
playing horses, two in front and one running behind
with the whip.

But—around the leg of the driver was knotted a
small white handkerchief and, sprawling across the
grass, as though someone had dropped it as they ran,
was a red-and-white checked scarf. At one end of it
was stitched a large white label bearing the initials—

M.P.

"So that's where she lost it!" said Michael, nodding his head wisely. "Shall we tell her we've found it?"

Jane glanced round. Mary Poppins was buttoning on her apron and looking as if the whole world had insulted her.

"Better not," she said, softly. "I expect she knows."

For a moment Jane stood there, gazing at the cracked Bowl, the knotted handkerchief and the scarf.

Then with a wild rush she ran across the room and flung herself upon the starched white figure.

"Oh," she cried, "oh, Mary Poppins! I'll never be naughty again."

A faint smile twinkled at the corners of Mary Poppins' mouth as she smoothed out the creases from her apron.

"Humph!" was all she said. . . .

4

TOPSY-TURVY

"KEEP CLOSE to me, please!" said Mary Poppins, stepping out of the Bus and putting up her umbrella, for it was raining heavily.

Jane and Michael scrambled out after her.

"If I keep close to you the drips from your umbrella run down my neck," complained Michael.

"Don't blame me, then, if you get lost and have to ask a Policeman!" snapped Mary Poppins, as she neatly avoided a puddle.

She paused outside the Chemist's shop at the corner so that she could see herself reflected in the three gigantic bottles in the window. She could see a Green Mary Poppins, a Blue Mary Poppins and a Red Mary Poppins all at once. And each one of them was carrying a brand-new leather handbag with brass knobs on it.

Mary Poppins looked at herself in the three bottles and smiled a pleased and satisfied smile. She spent some minutes changing the hand-bag from her right hand to her left, trying it in every possible position to see how it looked best. Then she decided that, after all, it was most effective when tucked under her arm. So she left it there.

Jane and Michael stood beside her, not daring to

say anything but glancing across at each other and sighing inside themselves. And from two points of her parrot-handled umbrella the rain trickled uncomfortably down the backs of their necks.

"Now then—don't keep me waiting!" said Mary
Poppins crossly, turning away from the Green, Blue
and Red reflections of herself. Jane and Michael exchanged glances. Jane signalled to Michael to keep
quiet. She shook her head and made a face at him.
But he burst out——

"We weren't. It was you keeping us waiting——!"

"Silence!"

Michael did not dare to say any more. He and
Jane trudged along, one on either side of Mary Poppins. Sometimes they had to run to keep up with her
long, swift strides. And sometimes they had to wait
about, standing first on one leg and then on the
other, while she peered into a window to make sure
the hand-bag looked as nice as she thought it did.

The rain poured down, dancing from the top of
the umbrella on to Jane's and Michael's hats. Under
her arm Jane carried the Royal Doulton Bowl
wrapped carefully in two pieces of paper. They were
taking it to Mary Poppins' cousin, Mr. Turvy, whose
business, she had told Mrs. Banks, was mending
things.

"Well," Mrs. Banks had said, rather doubtfully,
"I hope he will do it satisfactorily, for until it is
mended I shall not be able to look my Great-Aunt
Caroline in the face."

Great-Aunt Caroline had given Mrs. Banks the
bowl when Mrs. Banks was only three and it was
well-known that if it were broken Great-Aunt Caroline would make one of her famous scenes.

"Members of *my* family, ma'am," Mary Poppins
had retorted with a sniff, "*always* gives satisfaction."

And she had looked so fierce that Mrs. Banks felt quite uncomfortable and had to sit down and ring for a cup of tea.

Swish!

There was Jane, right in the middle of a puddle.

"Look where you're going, please!" snapped Mary Poppins, shaking her umbrella and tossing the drips over Jane and Michael. "This rain is enough to break your heart."

"If it did, could Mr. Turvy mend it?" enquired Michael. He was interested to know if Mr. Turvy could mend all broken things or only certain kinds. "Could he, Mary Poppins?"

"One more word," said Mary Poppins, "and Back Home you go!"

"I only asked," said Michael sulkily.

"Then don't!"

Mary Poppins, with an angry sniff, turned the corner smartly and, opening an old iron gate, knocked at the door of a small tumble-down building.

"Tap-tap-tappity-tap!" The sound of the knocker echoed hollowly through the house.

"Oh, dear," Jane whispered to Michael, "how awful if he's out!"

But at that moment heavy footsteps were heard tramping towards them and with a loud rattle, the door opened.

A round, red-faced woman, looking more like two apples placed one on top of the other than a human being, stood in the doorway. Her straight hair was scraped into a knob at the top of her head and her thin mouth had a cross and peevish expression.

"Well!" she said, staring. "It's you or I'm a Dutch-man!"

She did not seem particularly pleased to see Mary Poppins. Nor did Mary Poppins seem particularly pleased to see her.

"Is Mr. Turvy in?" she enquired, without taking any notice of the round woman's remark.

"Well," said the round woman in an unfriendly voice, "I wouldn't be certain. He may be or he may not. It's all a matter of how you look at it."

Mary Poppins stepped through the door and peered about her.

"That's his hat, isn't it?" she demanded, pointing to an old felt hat that hung on a peg in the hall.

"Well, it is, of course—in a manner of speaking." The round woman admitted the fact unwillingly.

"Then he's in," said Mary Poppins. "No member of *my* family ever goes out without a hat. They're much too respectable."

"Well, all I can tell you is what he said to me this morning," said the round woman. "'Miss Tartlet,' he said, 'I may be in this afternoon and I may not. It is quite impossible to tell.' That's what he said. But you'd better go up and see for yourself. I'm not a mountaineer."

The round woman glanced down at her round body and shook her head. Jane and Michael could easily understand that a person of her size and shape would not want to climb up and down Mr. Turvy's narrow ricketty stairs very often.

Mary Poppins sniffed.

"Follow me, please!" she snapped the words at

Jane and Michael and they ran after her up the creaking stairs.

Miss Tartlet stood in the hall watching them with a superior smile on her face.

At the top landing Mary Poppins knocked on the door with the head of her umbrella. There was no reply. She knocked again—louder this time. Still there was no answer.

"Cousin Arthur!" she called through the key-hole. "Cousin Arthur, are you in?"

"No, I'm out!" came a far-away voice from within.

"How can he be out? I can hear him!" whispered Michael to Jane.

"Cousin Arthur!" Mary Poppins rattled the door-handle. "I know you're in."

"No, no, I'm not," came the far-away voice. "I'm out, I tell you. It's the Second Monday!"

"Oh, dear—I'd forgotten!" said Mary Poppins, and with an angry movement she turned the handle and flung open the door.

At first all that Jane and Michael could see was a large room that appeared to be quite empty except for a carpenter's bench at one end. Piled upon this was a curious collection of articles—china dogs with no noses, wooden horses that had lost their tails, chipped plates, broken dolls, knives without handles, stools with only two legs—everything in the world, it seemed, that could possibly want mending.

Round the walls of the room were shelves reaching from floor to ceiling and these, too, were crowded with cracked china, broken glass and shattered toys.

But there was no sign anywhere of a human being.

"Oh," said Jane in a disappointed voice. "He *is* out, after all!"

But Mary Poppins had darted across the room to the window.

"Come in at once, Arthur! Out in the rain like that, and you with bronchitis the winter before last!"

And to their amazement Jane and Michael saw her grasp a long leg that hung across the window-sill and pull in from the outer air a tall, thin, sad-looking man with a long drooping moustache.

"You ought to be ashamed of yourself," said Mary Poppins crossly, keeping a firm hold of Mr. Turvy with one hand while she shut the window with the other. "We've brought you some important work to do and here you are behaving like this."

"Well, I can't help it," said Mr. Turvy apologetically, mopping his sad eyes with a large handkerchief. "I told you it was the Second Monday."

"What does that mean?" asked Michael, staring at Mr. Turvy with interest.

"Ah," said Mr. Turvy turning to him and shaking him limply by the hand. "It's kind of you to enquire. Very kind. I do appreciate it, really." He paused to wipe his eyes again. "You see," he went on, "it's this way. On the Second Monday of the month everything goes wrong with me."

"What kind of things?" asked Jane, feeling very sorry for Mr. Turvy but also very curious.

"Well, take to-day!" said Mr. Turvy. "This happens to be the Second Monday of the month. And because I want to be in—having so much work to do—

I'm automatically out. And if I wanted to be out, sure enough, I'd be in."

"I see," said Jane, though she really found it very difficult to understand. "So that's why——?"

"Yes," Mr. Turvy nodded. "I heard you coming up the stairs and I did so long to be in. So, of course, as soon as that happened—there I was—out! And I'd be out still if Mary Poppins weren't holding on to me." He sighed heavily.

"Of course, it's not like this all the time. Only between the hours of three and six—but even then it can be very awkward."

"I'm sure it can," said Jane sympathetically.

"And it's not as if it was only In and Out——" Mr. Turvy went on miserably. "It's other things, too. If I try to go up stairs, I find myself running down. I have only to turn to the right and I find myself going to the left. And I never set off for the West without immediately finding myself in the East."

Mr. Turvy blew his nose.

"And worst of all," he continued, his eyes filling again with tears, "my whole nature alters. To look at me now, you'd hardly believe I was really a happy and satisfied sort of person—would you?"

And, indeed, Mr. Turvy looked so melancholy and distressed that it seemed quite impossible he could ever have been cheerful and contented.

"But why? Why?" demanded Michael, staring up at him.

Mr. Turvy shook his head sadly.

"Ah!" he said solemnly. "I should have been a girl."

Jane and Michael stared at him and then at each other. What *could* he mean?

"You see," Mr. Turvy explained, "my Mother wanted a girl and it turned out, when I arrived, that I was a boy. So I went wrong right from the beginning—from the day I was born you might say. And that was the Second Monday of the month."

Mr. Turvy began to weep again, sobbing gently into his handkerchief.

Jane patted his hand kindly.

He seemed pleased, though he did not smile.

"And, of course," he went on, "It's very bad for my work. Look up there!"

He pointed to one of the larger shelves on which were standing a row of hearts in different colours and sizes, each one cracked or chipped or entirely broken.

"Now, those," said Mr. Turvy, "are wanted in a great hurry. You don't know how cross people get if I don't send their hearts back quickly. They make more fuss about them than anything else. And I simply daren't touch them till after six o'clock. They'd be ruined—like those things!"

He nodded to another shelf. Jane and Michael looked and saw that it was piled high with things that had been wrongly mended. A china shepherdess had been separated from her china shepherd and her arms were glued about the neck of a brass lion; a toy sailor whom somebody had wrenched from his boat, was firmly stuck to a willow-pattern plate; and in the boat, with his trunk curled round the mast and fixed there with sticking-plaster, was a grey-

flannel elephant. Broken saucers were riveted together the wrong way of the pattern and the leg of
a wooden horse was firmly attached to a silver Christening mug.

"You see?" said Mr. Turvy hopelessly, with a wave
of his hand.

Jane and Michael nodded. They felt very, very
sorry for Mr. Turvy.

"Well, never mind that now," Mary Poppins broke
in impatiently. "What is important is this Bowl.
We've brought it to be mended."

She took the Bowl from Jane and, still holding
Mr. Turvy with one hand, she undid the string with
the other.

"H'm," said Mr. Turvy. "Royal Doulton. A bad
crack. Looks as though somebody had thrown something at it."

Jane felt herself blushing as he said that.

"Still," he went on, "if it were any other day, I
could mend it. But to-day——" he hesitated.

"Nonsense, it's quite simple. You've only to put
a rivet here—and here—and here!"

Mary Poppins pointed to the crack and as she did
so she dropped Mr. Turvy's hand.

Immediately he went spinning through the air,
turning over and over like a Catherine wheel.

"Oh!" cried Mr. Turvy. "Why did you let go?
Poor me, I'm off again!"

"Quick—shut the door!" cried Mary Poppins. And
Jane and Michael rushed across the room and closed
the door just before Mr. Turvy reached it. He
banged against it and bounced away again, turning

gracefully, with a very sad look on his face, through the air.

Suddenly he stopped but in a very curious position. Instead of being right side up he was upside down and standing on his head.

"Dear, dear!" said Mr. Turvy, giving a fierce kick with his feet, "Dear, dear!"

But his feet would not go down to the floor. They remained waving gently in the air.

"Well," Mr. Turvy remarked in his melancholy voice. "I suppose I should be glad it's no worse. This is certainly better—though not *much* better—than hanging outside in the rain with nothing to sit on and no overcoat. You see," he looked at Jane and Michael, "I want so much to be right-side up and so—just my luck!—I'm upside down. Well, well, never mind. I ought to be used to it by now. I've had forty-five years of it. Give me the Bowl."

Michael ran and took the Bowl from Mary Poppins and put it on the floor by Mr. Turvy's head. And as he did so he felt a curious thing happening to him. The floor seemed to be pushing his feet away from it and tilting them into the air.

"Oh!" he cried. "I feel so funny. Something most extraordinary is happening to me!"

For by now he, too, was turning Catherine wheels through the air, and flying up and down the room until he landed head first on the floor beside Mr. Turvy.

"Strike me pink!" said Mr. Turvy in a surprised voice, looking at Michael out of the corner of his eye. "I never knew it was catching. You, too? Well, of all the—Hi! Hi, I say! Steady there! You'll knock the goods off the shelves, if you're not careful, and I shall be charged for breakages. What *are* you doing?"

He was now addressing Jane whose feet had suddenly swept off the carpet and were turning above her head in the giddiest manner. Over and over she went—first her head and then her feet in the air—until at last she came down on the other side of Mr. Turvy and found herself standing on her head.

"You know," said Mr. Turvy staring at her solemnly. "This is all very odd. I never knew it happen to any one else before. Upon my word, I never did. I do hope you don't mind."

Jane laughed, turning her head towards him and waving her legs in the air.

"Not a bit, thank you. I've always wanted to stand on my head and I've never been able to do it before. It's very comfortable."

"H'm," said Mr. Turvy dolefully. "I'm glad somebody likes it. I can't say *I* feel like that."

"I do," said Michael. "I wish I could stay like this all my life. Everything looks so nice and different."

And, indeed, everything *was* different. From their strange position on the floor Jane and Michael could see that the articles on the carpenter's bench were all upside down—china dogs, broken dolls, wooden stools —all standing on their heads.

"Look!" whispered Jane to Michael. He turned his head as much as he could. And there, creeping out of a hole in the wainscoting, came a small mouse. It skipped, head over heels, into the middle of the room and, turning upside down, balanced daintily on its nose in front of them.

They watched it for a moment, very surprised. Then Michael suddenly said,

"Jane, look out of the window!"

She turned her head carefully for it was rather difficult and saw to her astonishment that everything outside the room, as well as everything in it, was different. Out in the street the houses were standing on their heads, their chimneys on the pavement and their door-steps in the air and out of the door-steps came little curls of smoke. In the distance a church had turned turtle and was balancing rather top-heavily on the point of its steeple. And the rain, which had always seemed to them to come down from the sky, was pouring up from the earth in a steady soaking shower.

"Oh," said Jane. "How beautifully strange it all is! It's like being in another world. I'm so glad we came to-day."

"Well," said Mr. Turvy, mournfully, "you're very kind, I must say. You do know how to make allowances. Now, what about this Bowl?"

He stretched out his hand to take it but at that moment the Bowl gave a little skip and turned upside down. And it did it so quickly and so funnily that Jane and Michael could not help laughing.

"This," said Mr. Turvy miserably, "is no laughing matter for me, I assure you. I shall have to put the rivets in wrong way up—and if they show, they show. I can't help it."

And taking his tools out of his pocket he mended the Bowl, weeping quietly as he worked.

"Humph!" said Mary Poppins, stooping to pick it up. "Well, that's done. And now we'll be going."

At that Mr. Turvy began to sob pitifully.

"That's right, leave me!" he said bitterly. "Don't stay and help me keep my mind off my misery. Don't hold out a friendly hand. I'm not worth it. I'd hoped you might all favour me by accepting some refreshment. There's a plum cake in a tin up there on the top shelf. But, there—I'd no right to expect it. You've your own lives to live and I shouldn't ask you to stay and brighten mine. This isn't my lucky day——"

He fumbled for his pocket-handkerchief.

"Well——," began Mary Poppins, pausing in the middle of buttoning her gloves.

"Oh, do stay, Mary Poppins, do!" cried Jane and Michael together, dancing eagerly on their heads.

"You could reach the cake if you stood on a chair!" said Jane, helpfully.

Mr. Turvy laughed for the first time. It was rather a melancholy sound, but still, it *was* a laugh.

"*She'll* need no chair!" he said, gloomily chuckling in his throat. "She'll get what she wants and in the way she wants it—*she* will."

And at that moment, before the children's astonished eyes, Mary Poppins did a curious thing. She raised herself stiffly on her toes and balanced there for a moment. Then, very slowly, and in a most dignified manner she turned seven Catherine wheels through the air. Over and over, her skirts clinging neatly about her ankles, her hat set tidily on her head, she wheeled up to the top of the shelf, took the cake and wheeled down again, landing neatly on her head in front of Mr. Turvy and the children.

"Hooray! Hooray! Hooray!" shouted Michael delightedly. But from the floor Mary Poppins gave him such a look that he rather wished he had remained quiet and said nothing.

"Thank you, Mary," said Mr. Turvy sadly, not seeming at all surprised.

"There!" snapped Mary Poppins. "That's the last thing I shall do for you to-day."

She put the cake-tin down in front of Mr. Turvy. Immediately, with a little wobbly roll, it turned

"*Mary Poppins landed neatly on her head in front of
Mr. Turvy and the children*"

upside down. And each time Mr. Turvy turned it right side up it turned over again.

"Ah," he said despairingly, "I might have known it! Nothing is right to-day—not even the cake-tin. We shall have to cut it open from the bottom. I'll just ask——"

And he stumbled on his head to the door and shouted through the crack between it and the floor.

"Miss Tartlet! Miss Tartlet! I'm so sorry to trouble you, but could you—would you—do you mind bringing a tin-opener?"

Far away downstairs Miss Tartlet's voice could be heard grimly protesting.

"Tush!" said a loud croaky voice inside the room. "Tush and nonsense! Don't bother the woman! Let Polly do it! Pretty polly! Clever Polly!"

Turning their heads, Jane and Michael were surprised to see that the voice came from Mary Poppins' parrot-headed umbrella which was at that moment Catherine-wheeling towards the cake. It landed head downwards on the tin and in two seconds had cut a large hole in it with its beak.

"There!" squawked the parrot-head conceitedly, "Polly did it! Handsome Polly!" And a happy self-satisfied smile spread over its beak as it settled head-downwards on the floor beside Mary Poppins.

"Well, that's very kind, *very* kind," said Mr. Turvy in his gloomy voice, as the dark crust of the cake became visible.

He took a knife out of his pocket and cut a slice. He started violently, and peered at the cake more closely. Then he looked reproachfully at Mary Poppins.

"This is your doing, Mary! Don't deny it. That cake, when the tin was last open, was a plum cake and now——"

"Sponge is much more digestible," said Mary Poppins, primly. "Eat slowly please. You're not starving savages!" she snapped, passing a small slice each to Jane and Michael.

"That's all very well," grumbled Mr. Turvy bitterly, eating his slice in two bites. "But I do like a plum or two, I must admit. Ah, well, this is not my lucky day!" He broke off as somebody rapped loudly on the door. "Come in!" called Mr. Turvy.

Miss Tarlet, looking, if anything, rounder than ever and panting from her climb up the stairs, burst into the room.

"The tin-opener, Mr. Turvy——" she began grimly. Then she paused and stared.

"My!" she said, opening her mouth very wide and letting the tin-opener slip from her hand. "Of all the sights I ever did see this is the one I wouldn't have expected!"

She took a step forward, gazing at the four pairs of waving feet with an expression of deep disgust.

"Upside down—the lot of you—like flies on a ceiling! And you supposed to be respectable human creatures. This is no place for a lady of *my* standing. I shall leave the house this instant, Mr. Turvy. Please note that!"

She flounced angrily towards the door.

But even as she went her great billowing skirts

blew against her round legs and lifted her from the floor.

A look of agonised astonishment spread over her face. She flung out her hands wildly.

"Mr. Turvy! Mr. Turvy, Sir! Catch me! Hold me down! Help! Help!" cried Miss Tartlet as she, too, began a sweeping Catherine wheel.

"Oh, oh, the world's turning turtle! What shall I do? Help! Help!" she shrieked, as she went over again.

But as she turned a curious change came over her. Her round face lost its peevish expression and began to shine with smiles. And Jane and Michael, with a start of surprise, saw her straight hair crinkle into a mass of little curls and ringlets as she whirled and twirled through the room. When she spoke again her gruff voice was as sweet as honeysuckle.

"What can be happening to me?" cried Miss Tartlet's new voice. "I feel like a ball! A bouncing ball! Or perhaps a balloon! Or a cherry tart!" She broke into a peal of happy laughter.

"Dear me, how cheerful I am!" she trilled, turning and circling through the air. "I never enjoyed my life before but now I feel I shall never stop. It's the loveliest sensation. I shall write home to my sister about it, to my cousins and uncles and aunts. I shall tell them that the only proper way to live is upside down, upside down, upside down——"

And, chanting happily, Miss Tartlet went whirling round and round. Jane and Michael watched her with delight and Mr. Turvy watched her with

surprise, for he had never known Miss Tartlet to be
anything but peevish and unfriendly.

"Very odd! Very odd!" said Mr. Turvy to himself,
shaking his head as he stood on it.

Another knock sounded at the door.

"Anyone here name of Turvy?" enquired a voice,
and the Post Man appeared in the doorway holding
a letter. He stood staring at the sight that met his
eyes.

"Holy smoke!" he remarked, pushing his cap to
the back of his head. "I must-a come to the wrong
place. I'm looking for a decent quiet gentleman
called Turvy. I've got a letter for him. Besides, I
promised my wife I'd be home early and I've broken
my word and I thought——"

"Ha!" said Mr. Turvy from the floor. "A broken
promise is one of the things I can't mend. Not my
line. Sorry!"

The Post Man stared down at him.

"Am I dreaming or am I not?" he muttered. "It
seems to me I've got into a whirling, twirling, skirling
company of lunatics!"

"Give me the letter, dear Post Man! Give the letter to Topsy Tartlet and turn upside down with me.
Mr. Turvy, you see, is engaged!"

Miss Tartlet, wheeling towards the Post Man, took
his hand in hers. And as she touched him his feet
slithered off the floor into the air. Then away they
went, the Post Man and Miss Tartlet, hand in hand
and over and over, like a pair of bouncing foot-balls.
"How lovely it is!" cried Miss Tartlet happily. "Oh,
Post Man dear, we're seeing life for the first time.

And such a pleasant view of it! Over we go! Isn't it wonderful?"

"Yes!" shouted Jane and Michael, as they joined the wheeling dance of the Post Man and Miss Tartlet.

And presently Mr. Turvy, too, joined in, awkwardly turning and tossing through the air. Mary Poppins and her umbrella followed, going over and over evenly and neatly and with the utmost dignity. There they all were, spinning and wheeling, with the world going up and down outside and the happy cries of Miss Tartlet echoing through the room.

> "The whole of the Town
> Is Upside Down!"

she sang, bouncing and bounding.

And up on the shelves the cracked and broken hearts twirled and spun like tops, the shepherdess and her lion waltzed gracefully together, the grey-flannel elephant stood on his trunk in the boat and kicked his feet in the air, and the toy sailor danced a hornpipe, not on his feet but his head, which bobbed about the willow-pattern plate very gracefully.

"How happy I am!" cried Jane as she careered across the room.

"How happy *I* am!" cried Michael, turning somersaults in the air.

Mr. Turvy mopped his eyes with his handkerchief as he bounced off the window pane.

Mary Poppins and her umbrella said nothing but just sailed calmly round, head downwards.

"How happy we *all* are!" cried Miss Tartlet.

But the Post Man had now found his tongue and
he did not agree with her.

"'Ere!" he shouted, turning again. "'Elp! 'Elp!

Where am I? Who am I? What am I? I don't know
at all. I'm lost! Oh, 'elp!"

But nobody helped him and firmly held in Miss
Tartlet's grasp he was whirled on.

"Always lived a quiet life—I have!" he moaned.
"Behaved like a decent citizen, too. Oh, what'll my

wife say! And 'ow shall I get 'ome? 'Elp! Fire! Thieves!"

And making a great effort, he wrenched his hand violently from Miss Tartlet's. He dropped the letter into the cake tin and went wheeling out of the door and down the stairs, head over heels, crying loudly—

"I'll have the law on them! I'll call the Police! I'll speak to the Post Master General!"

His voice died away as he went bounding further down the stairs.

"Ping, Ping, ping, ping, ping, ping!"

The clock outside in the Square sounded six.

And at the same moment Jane's and Michael's feet came down to the floor with a thud and they stood up feeling rather giddy.

Mary Poppins gracefully turned right side up, looking as smart and tidy as a figure in a shop window.

The Umbrella wheeled over and stood on its point.

Mr. Turvy, with a great tossing of legs, scrambled to his feet.

The hearts on the shelf stood still and steady and no movement came from the shepherdess or the lion, or the grey-flannel elephant or the toy sailor. To look at them you would never have guessed that a moment before they had all been dancing on their heads.

Only Miss Tartlet went whirling on, round and round the room, feet over head, laughing happily and singing her song.

"The whole of the Town
Is Upside down,
Upside down,
Upside down!"

she chanted joyfully.

"Miss Tartlet! Miss Tartlet!" cried Mr. Turvy,
running towards her, a strange light in his eyes. He
took her arm as she wheeled past and held it tightly
until she stood up on her feet beside him.

"*What* did you say your name was?" said Mr.
Turvy, panting with excitement.

Miss Tartlet actually blushed. She looked at him
shyly.

"Why, Tartlet, sir. Topsy Tartlet!"

Mr. Turvy took her hand.

"Then will you marry me, Miss Tartlet, and be
Topsy Turvy? It would make up to me for so much.
And you seem to have become so happy that perhaps
you will be kind enough to overlook my Second
Mondays."

"Overlook them, Mr. Turvy? Why, they will be
my Greatest Treats," said Miss Tartlet. "I have seen
the world upside down to-day and I have got a New
Point of View. I assure you I shall look forward to
the Second Mondays all the month!"

She laughed shyly and gave Mr. Turvy her other
hand. And Mr. Turvy, Jane and Michael were glad
to see, laughed too.

"It's after six o'clock, so I suppose he can be himself again!" whispered Michael to Jane.

Jane did not answer. She was watching the Mouse.

It was no longer standing on its nose but hurrying away to its hole with a large crumb of cake in its mouth.

Mary Poppins picked up the Royal Doulton Bowl and proceeded to wrap it up.

"Pick up your handkerchiefs, please—and straighten your hats," she snapped.

"And now——" she took her umbrella and tucked her new bag under her arm.

"Oh, we're not going yet, are we, Mary Poppins?" said Michael.

"If *you* are in the habit of staying out all night, I am not," she remarked, pushing him towards the door.

"Must you go, really?" said Mr. Turvy. But he seemed to be saying it out of mere politeness. He had eyes only for Miss Tartlet.

But Miss Tartlet herself came up to them, smiling radiantly and tossing her curls.

"Come again," she said, giving a hand to each of them. "Now, do. Mr. Turvy and I——" she looked down shyly and blushed—"will be in to tea every Second Monday—won't we, Arthur?"

"Well," said Mr. Turvy, "we'll be in if we're not out—I'm sure of that!" And he laughed and Jane and Michael laughed.

And he and Miss Tartlet stood at the top of the stairs waving good-bye to Mary Poppins and the children, Miss Tartlet blushing happily and Mr. Turvy holding Miss Tartlet's hand and looking very proud and pompous. . . .

"I didn't know it was as easy as that," said Michael to Jane as they splashed through the rain, under Mary Poppins' umbrella.

"What was?" said Jane.

"Standing on my head. I shall practise it when I get home."

"I wish *we* could have Second Mondays," said Jane dreamily.

"Get in, please!" said Mary Poppins, shutting her umbrella and pushing the children up the winding stairs of the bus.

They sat together in the seat behind her, talking quietly about all that had happened that afternoon.

Mary Poppins turned and glared at them.

"It is rude to whisper," she said fiercely. "And sit up straight. You're not flour-bags!"

They were quiet for a few minutes. Mary Poppins, half-turning in her seat, watched them with angry eyes.

"What a funny family you've got," Michael remarked to her, trying to make conversation.

Her head went up with a jerk.

"Funny? What do you mean, pray—funny?"

"Well—odd. Mr. Turvy turning Catherine wheels and standing on his head——"

Mary Poppins stared at him as though she could not believe her ears.

"Did I understand you to say," she began, speaking her words as though she were biting them, "that my cousin turned a Catherine wheel? And stood on——"

"But he did," protested Michael nervously. "We saw him"

"On his head? A relation of mine on his head? And turning about like a firework display?" Mary Poppins seemed hardly able to repeat the dreadful statement. She glared at Michael.

"Now this——" she began and he shrank back in terror from her wild darting eyes. "This is the Last Straw. First you are impudent to me and then you insult my relations. It would take very little more—Very Little More—to make me give notice. So—I warn you!"

And with that she bounced round on her seat and sat with her back to them. And even from the back she looked angrier than they had ever seen her.

Michael leaned forward.

"I—I apologise," he said.

There was no answer from the seat in front.

"I'm sorry, Mary Poppins!"

"Humph!"

"*Very* sorry!"

"And well you might be!" she retorted, staring straight ahead of her.

Michael leant towards Jane.

"But it was true—what I said. Wasn't it?" he whispered.

Jane shook her head and put her finger to her lip. She was staring at Mary Poppins' hat. And presently, when she was sure that Mary Poppins was not looking, she pointed to the brim.

There, gleaming on the black shiny straw, was a scattering of crumbs, yellow crumbs from a sponge cake, the kind of thing you would expect to find on the hat of a person who had stood on their head to have tea.

Michael gazed at the crumbs for a moment. Then he turned and nodded understandingly to Jane.

They sat there, jogging up and down as the bus rumbled homewards. Mary Poppins' back, erect and angry, was like a silent warning. They dared not speak to her. But every time the bus turned a corner they saw the crumbs turning Catherine wheels on the shining brim of her hat. . . .

5

THE NEW ONE

"**B**UT *why* must we go for a walk with Ellen?" grumbled Michael, slamming the gate. "I don't like her. Her nose is too red."

"Sh!" said Jane. "She'll hear you."

Ellen who was wheeling the perambulator, turned round.

"You're a cruel, unkind boy, Master Michael. I'm only doing my duty, I'm sure! It's no pleasure to me to be going for a walk in this heat—so there!"

She blew her red nose on a green handkerchief.

"Then why do you go?" Michael demanded.

"Because Mary Poppins is busy. So come along, there's a good boy, and I'll buy you a pennorth of peppermints."

"I don't want peppermints," muttered Michael. "I want Mary Poppins."

Plop-plop. Plop-plop. Ellen's feet marched slowly and heavily along the Lane.

"I can see a rainbow through every chink of my hat," said Jane.

"I can't," said Michael crossly. "I can only see my silk lining."

Ellen stopped at the corner, looking anxiously for traffic.

"Want any help?" enquired the Policeman, sauntering up to her.

"Well," said Ellen, blushing, "if you could take us across the road, I'd be much obliged. What with a bad cold, and four children to look after, I don't know if I'm on my head or my feet." She blew her nose again.

"But you *must* know! You've only got to look!" said Michael thinking how Perfectly Awful Ellen was.

But the Policeman apparently thought differently for he took Ellen's arm with one hand, and the handle of the perambulator with the other, and led her across the street as tenderly as though she were a bride.

"Ever get a day off?" he enquired, looking interestedly into Ellen's red face.

"Well," said Ellen. "Half-days, so to speak. Every second Saturday." She blew her nose nervously.

"Funny," said the Policeman. "Those are *my* days, too. And I'm usually just around here at two o'clock in the afternoon."

"Oh!" said Ellen, opening her mouth very wide.

"So!" said the Policeman, nodding at her politely.

"Well, I'll see," said Ellen. "Good-bye."

And she went trudging on, looking back occasionally to see if the Policeman was still looking.

And he always was.

Mary Poppins never needs a policeman," complained Michael. "What *can* she be busy about?"

"Something important is happening at home," said Jane. "I'm sure of it."

"How do you know?"

"I've got an empty, waiting sort of feeling inside."

"Pooh!" said Michael. "I expect you're hungry! Can't we go faster, Ellen, and get it over?"

"That boy," said Ellen to the Park railing, "has a heart of stone. No, we can't, Master Michael, because of my feet."

"What's the matter with them?"

"They will only go so fast and no faster."

"Oh, *dear* Mary Poppins!" said Michael bitterly.

He went sighing after the perambulator. Jane walked beside him counting rainbows through her hat.

Ellen's slow feet tramped steadily onward. One-two. One-two. Plop-plop. Plop-plop. . . .

And away behind them in Cherry Tree Lane the important thing was happening.

From the outside, Number Seventeen looked as peaceful and sleepy as all the other houses. But behind the drawn blinds there was such a stir and bustle that, if it hadn't been Summer-time, a passer-by might have thought the people in the house were Spring-cleaning or getting ready for Christmas.

But the house itself stood blinking in the sunshine, taking no notice. After all, it thought to itself, I have seen such bustlings often before and shall probably see them many times again, so why should *I* bother about it?

And just then, the front door was flung open by Mrs. Brill and Doctor Simpson hurried out. Mrs. Brill stood dancing on her toes as she watched him go down the garden path, swinging his little brown bag. Then she hurried to the Pantry and called excitedly——

"Where are you, Robertson? Come along, if you're coming!"

She scuttled up the stairs two at a time with Robertson Ay yawning and stretching, behind her.

"Sh!" hissed Mrs. Brill. "Sh!"

She put her finger to her lips and tip-toed to Mrs. Banks' door.

"Tch, tch! You can't see nothing but the wardrobe," she complained, as she bent to look through the key-hole. "The wardrobe and a bit of the winder."

But the next moment she started violently.

"My Glory-goodness!" she shrieked, as the door burst open suddenly, and she fell back against Robertson Ay.

For there, framed against the light, stood Mary Poppins, looking very stern and suspicious. In her arms she carried, with great care, something that looked like a bundle of blankets.

"Well!" said Mrs. Brill, breathlessly. "If it isn't you! I was just polishing the door-knob, putting a shine on it, so to say, as you came out."

Mary Poppins looked at the knob. It was very dirty.

"Polishing the key-hole is what *I* should have said!"
she remarked tartly.

But Mrs. Brill took no notice. She was gazing tenderly at the bundle. With her large red hand she
drew aside a fold of one of the blankets and a satisfied
smile spread over her face.

"Ah!" she cooed. "Ah, the Lamb! Ah, the Duck!
Ah, the Trinket! And as good as a week of Sundays,
I'll be bound!"

Robertson Ay yawned again and stared at the
bundle with his mouth slightly open.

"Another pair of shoes to clean!" he said mournfully, leaning against the banisters for support.

"Mind you don't drop it, now!" said Mrs. Brill
anxiously, as Mary Poppins brushed past her.

Mary Poppins glanced at them both contemptuously.

"If I were *some* people," she remarked acidly, "I'd
mind my own business!"

And she folded the blanket over the bundle again
and went upstairs to the Nursery.

"Excuse me, please! Excuse me!" Mr. Banks came
rushing up the stairs, nearly knocking Mrs. Brill over
as he hurried into Mrs. Banks' bedroom.

"Well!" he said, sitting down at the foot of the bed,
"This is all very awkward. Very awkward indeed. I
don't know that I can afford it. I hadn't bargained
for five."

"I'm so sorry!" said Mrs. Banks, smiling at him
happily.

"You're not sorry, not a bit. In fact you're very

pleased and conceited about it. And there's no reason to be. It's a very small one."

"I like them that way," said Mrs. Banks. "Besides, it will grow."

"Yes, unfortunately!" he replied bitterly. "And I shall have to buy it shoes and clothes and a tricycle. Yes, and send it to school and give it a Good Start in Life. A very expensive proceeding. And then, after all that, when I'm an old man sitting by the fire, it will go away and leave me. You hadn't thought of that, I suppose?"

"No," said Mrs. Banks, trying to look sorry but not succeeding. "I hadn't."

"I thought not. Well, there it is. But, I warn you, I shall not be able to afford to have the bathroom re-tiled."

"Don't worry about that," said Mrs. Banks comfortingly. "I really like the old tiles best."

"Then you're a very stupid woman. That's all I have to say."

And Mr. Banks went away, muttering and blustering through the house. But when he got outside the front door, he flung back his shoulders, and pushed out his chest, and put a large cigar into his mouth. And soon after that he was heard telling Admiral Boom the news in a voice that was very loud and conceited and boastful. . . .

Mary Poppins stooped over the new cradle between John's and Barbara's cots and laid the bundle of blankets carefully in it.

"Here you are at last! Bless my beak and tail feathers—— I thought you were never coming! Which is it?" cried a croaking voice from the window.

Mary Poppins looked up.

The Starling who lived on the top of the Chimney was hopping excitedly on the window-sill.

"A girl. Annabel," said Mary Poppins shortly. "And I'll thank you to be a little quieter. Squawking and croaking there like a packet of Magpies!"

But the Starling was not listening. He was turning somersaults on the window-sill, clapping his wings wildly together each time his head came up.

"What a treat!" he panted, when at last he stood up straight. "What a TREAT! Oh, I could sing!"

"You couldn't. Not if you tried till Doomsday!" scoffed Mary Poppins.

But the Starling was too happy to care.

"A girl!" he shrieked, dancing on his toes. "I've had three broods this season and—would you believe it?—every one of them boys. But Annabel will make up to me for that!"

He hopped a little along the sill. "Annabel!" he burst out again, "That's a nice name! I had an Aunt called Annabel. Used to live in Admiral Boom's chimney and died, poor thing, of eating green apples and grapes. I warned her, I warned her! But she wouldn't believe me! So, of course——"

"Will you be quiet!" demanded Mary Poppins, making a dive at him with her apron.

"I will not!" he shouted, dodging neatly. "This

is no time for silence. I'm going to spread the news."

He swooped out of the window.

"Back in five minutes!" he screamed at her over his shoulder, as he darted away.

Mary Poppins moved quietly about the Nursery, putting Annabel's new clothes in a neat pile.

The Sunlight, slipping in at the window, crept across the room and up to the cradle.

"Open your eyes!" it said softly. "And I'll put a shine on them!"

The coverlet of the cradle trembled. Annabel opened her eyes.

"Good girl!" said the Sunlight. "They're blue, I see. My favourite colour! There! You won't find a brighter pair of eyes anywhere!"

It slipped lightly out of Annabel's eyes and down the side of the cradle.

"Thank you very much!" said Annabel politely.

A warm Breeze stirred the muslin flounces at her head.

"Curls or straight?" it whispered, dropping into the cradle beside her.

"Oh, curls, please!" said Annabel softly.

"It does save trouble, doesn't it?" agreed the Breeze. And it moved over her head, carefully turning up the feathery edges of her hair, before it fluttered off across the room.

"Here we are! Here we are!"

A harsh voice shrilled from the window. The Starling had returned to the sill. And behind him, wobbling uncertainly as he alighted, came a very young bird.

Mary Poppins moved towards them threateningly.

"Now you be off!" she said angrily. "I'll have no sparrers littering up this Nursery——"

But the Starling, with the young one at his side, brushed haughtily past her.

"Kindly remember, Mary Poppins," he said icily, "that *all* my families are properly brought up. Littering, indeed!"

He alighted neatly on the edge of the cradle and steadied the Fledgling beside him.

The young bird stared about him with round, inquisitive eyes. The Starling hopped along to the pillow.

"Annabel, dear," he began, in a husky, wheedling voice, "I'm very partial to a nice, crisp, crunchy piece of Arrowroot Biscuit." His eyes twinkled greedily. "You haven't one about you, I suppose?"

The curled head stirred on the pillow.

"No? Well, you're young yet for biscuits, perhaps. Your sister Barbara—nice girl, she was, very generous and pleasant—always remembered me. So if, in the future, *you* could spare the old fellow a crumb or two——"

"Of course I will," said Annabel from the folds of the blanket.

"Good girl!" croaked the Starling approvingly. He cocked his head on one side and gazed at her with his round bright eye. "I hope," he remarked politely, "you are not too tired after your journey."

Annabel shook her head.

"Where has she come from—out of an egg?"
cheeped the Fledgling suddenly.

"Huh-huh!" scoffed Mary Poppins. "Do you think
she's a sparrer?"

The Starling gave her a pained and haughty look.

"Well, what is she, then? And where did she come
from?" cried the Fledgling shrilly, flapping his short
wings and staring down at the cradle.

"*You* tell him, Annabel!" the Starling croaked.

Annabel moved her hands inside the blanket.

"I am earth and air and fire and water," she said
softly. "I come from the Dark where all things have
their beginning."

"Ah, such dark!" said the Starling softly, bending
his head to his breast.

"It was dark in the egg, too," the Fledgling cheeped.

"I come from the sea and its tides," Annabel went on. "I come from the sky and its stars, I come from the sun and its brightness——"

"Ah, so bright!" said the Starling, nodding.

"And I come from the forests of earth."

As if in a dream, Mary Poppins rocked the cradle —to-and-fro, to-and-fro with a steady swinging movement.

"Yes?" whispered the Fledgling.

"Slowly I moved at first," said Annabel, "always sleeping and dreaming. I remembered all I had been and I thought of all I shall be. And when I had dreamed my dream I awoke and came swiftly."

She paused for a moment, her blue eyes full of memories.

"And then?" prompted the Fledgling.

"I heard the stars singing as I came and I felt warm wings about me. I passed the beasts of the jungle and, came through the dark, deep waters. It was a long journey."

Annabel was silent.

The Fledgling stared at her with his bright inquisitive eyes.

Mary Poppins' hand lay quietly on the side of the cradle. She had stopped rocking.

"A long journey, indeed!" said the Starling softly, lifting his head from his breast. "And, ah, so soon forgotten!"

Annabel stirred under the quilt.

"No!" she said confidently. "I'll never forget."

"Stuff and Nonsense! Beaks and Claws! Of course you will! By the time the week's out you won't remember a word of it—what you are or where you came from!"

Inside her flannel petticoat Annabel was kicking furiously.

"I will! I will! How could I forget?"

"Because they all do!" jeered the Starling harshly. "Every silly human except—" he nodded his head at Mary Poppins—"her! She's Different, she's the Oddity, she's the Misfit——"

"You Sparrer!" cried Mary Poppins, making a dart at him.

But with a rude laugh he swept his Fledgling off the edge of the cradle and flew with him to the window-sill.

"Tipped you last!" he said cheekily, as he brushed by. "Hullo, what's that?"

There was a chorus of voices outside on the landing and a clatter of feet on the stairs.

"I don't believe you! I won't believe you!" cried Annabel wildly.

And at that moment Jane and Michael and the Twins burst into the room.

"Mrs. Brill says you've got something to show us!" said Jane, flinging off her hat.

"What is it?" demanded Michael, gazing round the room.

"Show me! Me, too!" shrieked the Twins.

Mary Poppins glared at them. "Is this a decent nursery or the Zoological gardens?" she enquired angrily. "Answer me that!"

She sat down in the old armchair

"The Zoo—er—I mean——" Michael broke off hurriedly for he had caught Mary Poppins' eye. "I mean a Nursery," he said lamely.

"Oh, look, Michael, look!" Jane cried excitedly. "I told you something important was happening! It's a New Baby! Oh, Mary Poppins, can I have it to keep?"

Mary Poppins, with a furious glance at them all, stooped and lifted Annabel out of the cradle and sat down with her in the old arm-chair.

"Gently, please, gently!" she warned, as they crowded about her. "This is a baby, not a battleship!"

"A boy-baby?" asked Michael.

"No, a girl—Annabel."

Michael and Annabel stared at each other. He put his finger into her hand and she clutched it tightly.

"My doll!" said John, pushing up against Mary Poppins' knee.

"My rabbit!" said Barbara, tugging at Annabel's shawl.

"Oh!" breathed Jane, touching the hair that the wind had curled. "How very small and sweet. Like a star. Where *did* you come from, Annabel?"

Very pleased to be asked, Annabel began her story again.

"I came from the Dark——" she recited softly.

Jane laughed. "Such funny little sounds!" she cried. "I wish she could talk and tell us."

Annabel stared.

"But I *am* telling you," she protested, kicking.

"Ha-ha!" shrieked the Starling rudely from the window. "What did I say? Excuse me laughing!"

The Fledgling giggled behind his wing.

"Perhaps she came from a Toy-Shop," said Michael.

Annabel, with a furious movement, flung his finger from her.

"Don't be silly!" said Jane. "Doctor Simpson must have brought her in his little brown bag!"

"Was I right or was I wrong?" The Starling's old dark eyes gleamed tauntingly at Annabel.

"Tell me that!" he jeered, flapping his wings in triumph.

But for answer Annabel turned her face against Mary Poppins' apron and wept. Her first cries, thin and lonely, rang piercingly through the house.

"There! There!" said the Starling gruffly. "Don't take on! It can't be helped. You're only a human child after all. But next time, perhaps, you'll believe your Betters! Elders and Betters! Elders and Betters!" he screamed, prancing conceitedly up and down.

"Michael, take my feather duster please, and sweep those birds off the sill!" said Mary Poppins ominously.

A squawk of amusement came from the Starling.

"We can sweep ourselves off, Mary Poppins, thank you! We were just going, anyway! Come along, Boy!"

And with a loud clucking chuckle he flicked the Fledgling over the sill and swooped with him through the window. . . .

In a very short time, Annabel settled down comfortably to life in Cherry Tree Lane. She enjoyed being the centre of attraction and was always pleased when somebody leant over her cradle and said how pretty she was, or how good or sweet-tempered.

"Do go on admiring me!" she would say, smiling. "I like it so much!"

And then they would hasten to tell her how curly her hair was and how blue her eyes, and Annabel would smile in such a satisfied way that they would cry, "How intelligent she is! You would almost think. she understood!"

But *that* always annoyed her and she would turn away in disgust at their foolishness. Which was silly because when she was disgusted she looked so charming that they became more foolish than ever.

She was a week old before the Starling returned. Mary Poppins, in the dim glow of the night-light was gently rocking the cradle, when he appeared.

"Back again?" snapped Mary Poppins, watching him prance in. "You're as bad as a bad penny!" She gave a long disgusted sniff.

"I've been busy!" said the Starling. "Have to keep my affairs in order. And this isn't the *only* Nursery I have to look after, you know!" His beady black eyes twinkled wickedly.

"Humph!" she said shortly, "I'm sorry for the others!"

He chuckled, and shook his head.

"Nobody like her!" he remarked chirpily to the blind-tassel. "Nobody like her! She's got an answer for everything!" He cocked his head towards the cradle. "Well, how are things? Annabel asleep?"

"No thanks to you, if she is!" said Mary Poppins.

The Starling ignored the remark. He hopped to the end of the sill.

"I'll keep watch," he said, in a whisper. "You go down and get a cup of tea!"

Mary Poppins stood up.

"Mind you don't wake her, then!"

The Starling laughed pityingly.

"My dear girl, I have in my time brought up at least twenty broods of fledglings. I don't need to be told how to look after a mere baby."

"Humph!" Mary Poppins walked to the cupboard and very pointedly put the biscuit tin under her arm before she went out and shut the door.

The Starling marched up and down the windowsill, backwards and forwards, with his wing-tips under his tail-feathers.

There was a small stir in the cradle. Annabel opened her eyes.

"Hullo!" she said. "I was wanting to see you."

"Ha!" said the Starling, swooping across to her.

"There's something I wanted to remember," said Annabel frowning, "and I thought you might remind me."

He started. His dark eye glittered.

"How does it go?" he said softly. "Like this?"

And he began in a husky whisper—"I am earth and air and fire and water——"

"No, no!" said Annabel impatiently. "Of course it doesn't."

"Well," said the Starling anxiously. "Was it about your journey? You came from the sea and its tides, you came from the sky and——"

"Oh, don't be so *silly*!" cried Annabel. "The only journey I ever took was to the Park and back again this morning. No, no—it was something *important*. Something beginning with B."

She crowed suddenly.

"I've got it!" she cried. "It's Biscuit. Half-an Arrowroot Biscuit on the mantel-piece. Michael left it there after tea!"

"Is that all?" said the Starling sadly.

"Yes, of course," Annabel said fretfully. "Isn't it enough? I thought you'd be glad of a nice piece of biscuit!"

"So I am, so I am!" said the Starling hastily. "But——"

She turned her head on the pillow and closed her eyes.

"Don't talk any more now, please!" she said. "I want to go to sleep."

The Starling glanced across at the mantel-piece, and down again at Annabel.

"Biscuits!" he said, shaking his head. "Alas, Annabel, alas!"

Mary Poppins came in quietly and closed the door.

"Did she wake?" she said in a whisper.

The Starling nodded.

"Only for a minute," he said sadly. "But it was long enough."

Mary Poppins' eyes questioned him.

"She's forgotten," he said, with a catch in his croak.

"She's forgotten it all. I knew she would. But, ah, my dear, what a pity!"

"Humph!"

Mary Poppins moved quietly about the Nursery, putting the toys away. She glanced at the Starling. He was standing on the window-sill with his back to her and his speckled shoulders were heaving.

"Caught another cold?" she remarked sarcastically.

He wheeled around.

"Certainly not! It's—ahem—the night air. Rather chilly, you know. Makes the eyes water. Well—I must be off!"

He waddled unsteadily to the edge of the sill. "I'm getting old," he croaked sadly. "That's what it is! Not so young as we were. Eh, Mary Poppins?"

"I don't know about *you*——" Mary Poppins drew herself up haughtily. "But I'm *quite* as young as I was, thank you!"

"Ah," said the Starling, shaking his head. "You're a Wonder. An absolute, Marvellous, Wonderful Wonder!" His round eye twinkled wickedly.

"I don't think!" he called back rudely, as he dived out of the window.

"Impudent Sparrer!" she shouted after him and shut the window with a bang. . . .

6

ROBERTSON AY'S STORY

"STEP along, please!" said Mary Poppins, pushing the perambulator, with the Twins at one end of it and Annabel at the other, towards her favourite seat in the Park.

It was a green one, quite near the Lake, and she chose it because she could bend sideways, every now and again, and see her own reflection in the water. The sight of her face gleaming between two waterlilies always gave her a pleasant feeling of satisfaction and contentment.

Michael trudged behind.

"We're always stepping along," he grumbled to Jane in a whisper, taking care that Mary Poppins did not hear him, "but we never seem to get anywhere."

Mary Poppins turned round and glared at him.

"Put your hat on straight!"

Michael tilted his hat over his eyes. It had "H.M.S. Trumpeter" printed on the band and he thought it suited him very well.

But Mary Poppins was looking with contempt at them both.

"Humph!" she said. "You two look a picture, I must say! Stravaiging along like a couple of tortoises and no polish on your shoes."

"Well, it's Robertson Ay's Half-day," said Jane. "I suppose he didn't have time to do them before he went out."

"Tch, tch! Lazy, idle, Good-for-nothing—that's what he is. Always was and always will be!" Mary Poppins said, savagely pushing the perambulator up against her own green seat.

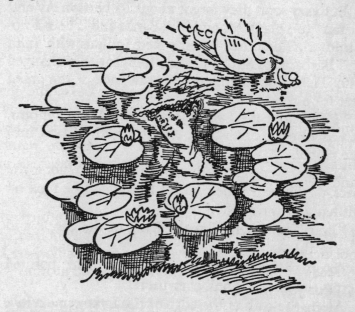

She lifted out the Twins, and tucked the shawl tightly around Annabel. She glanced at her sunlit reflection in the Lake and smiled in a superior way, straightening the new bow of ribbon at her neck. Then she took her bag of knitting from the perambulator.

"How do you know he's always been idle?" asked

Jane. "Did you know Robertson Ay before you came here?"

"Ask no questions and you'll be told no lies!" said Mary Poppins priggishly, as she began to cast on stitches for a woollen vest for John.

"She never tells us *anything!*" Michael grumbled.

"I know!" sighed Jane.

But very soon they forgot about Robertson Ay and began to play Mr-and-Mrs-Banks-and-Their-Two-Children. Then they became Red Indians with John and Barbara for Squaws. And after that they changed into Tight-Rope-Walkers with the back of the green seat for a rope.

"Mind my hat—*if* you please!" said Mary Poppins. It was a brown one with a pigeon's feather stuck into the ribbon.

Michael went carefully, foot over foot, along the back of the seat. When he got to the end he took off his hat and waved it.

"Jane," he cried, "I'm the King of the Castle and you're the——"

"Stop, Michael!" she interrupted and pointed across the Lake. "Look over there!"

Along the path at the edge of the Lake came a tall, slim figure, curiously dressed. He wore stockings of red striped with yellow, a red-and-yellow tunic scalloped at the edges and on his head was a large-brimmed red-and-yellow hat with a high peaked crown.

Jane and Michael watched with interest as he came towards them, moving with a lazy swaggering step, his hands in his pockets and his hat pulled down over his eyes.

He was whistling loudly and as he drew nearer they saw that the peaks of his tunic, and the brim of his hat, were edged with little bells that jingled musically as he moved. He was the strangest person they had ever seen and yet—there was something about him that seemed familiar.

"I think I've seen him before," said Jane, frowning and trying to remember.

"So have I. But I can't think where." Michael balanced on the back of the seat and stared.

Whistling and jingling, the curious figure slouched up to Mary Poppins and leaned against the perambulator.

"Day, Mary!" he said, putting a finger lazily to the brim of his hat. "And how are you keeping?"

Mary Poppins looked up from her knitting.

"None the better for your asking," she said, with a loud sniff.

Jane and Michael could not see the man's face for the brim of his hat was well pulled down, but from the way the bells jingled they knew he was laughing.

"Busy as usual, I see!" he remarked, glancing at the knitting. "But then, you always were, even at Court. If you weren't dusting the Throne you'd be making the King's bed, and if you weren't doing that you were polishing the Crown Jewels. I never knew such a one for work!"

"Well, it's more than anyone could say for you," said Mary Poppins crossly.

"Ah," laughed the Stranger, "that's just where

you're wrong! I'm always busy. Doing nothing takes
a great deal of time! All the time, in fact!"

Mary Poppins pursed up her lips and made no
reply.

The Stranger gave an amused chuckle. "Well, I
must be getting along." He said. "See you again some
day!"

He brushed a finger along the bells of his hat and
sauntered lazily away, whistling as he went.

Jane and Michael watched until he was out of
sight.

"The Dirty Rascal!"

Mary Poppins' voice rapped out behind them, and
they turned to find that she, too, was staring after the
Stranger.

"Who was that man, Mary Poppins?" asked Michael, bouncing excitedly up and down on the seat.

"I've just told you," she snapped. "You said you
were the King of the Castle—and you're not, not by
any means! But that's the Dirty Rascal."

"You mean the one in the Nursery Rhyme?"
demanded Jane breathlessly.

"But Nursery Rhymes aren't true, are they?" protested Michael. "And if they are, who *is* the King of
the Castle."

"Hush!" said Jane, laying her hand on his arm.

Mary Poppins had put down her knitting and was
gazing out across the Lake with a far-away look in
her eyes.

Jane and Michael sat very still hoping, if they made
no sound, she would tell them the whole story. The
Twins huddled together at one end of the peram-

bulator, solemnly staring at Mary Poppins. Annabel,
at the other end, was sound asleep.

"The King of the Castle," began Mary Poppins,
folding her hands over her ball of wool and gazing
right through the children as though they were not
there. "The King of the Castle lived in a country so
far away that most people have never heard of it.
Think as far as you can, and it's even further than
that; think as high as you can, and it's higher than
that; think as deep as you can, and it's even deeper.

"And," she said, "if I were to tell you how rich
he was we'd be sitting here till next year and still be
only half-way through the list of his treasures. He was
enormously, preposterously, extravagantly rich. In
fact, there was only one thing in the whole world
that he did not possess.

"And that thing was wisdom."

And so Mary Poppins went on——

His land was full of gold mines, his people were
polite and prosperous and generally splenderiferous.
He had a good wife and four fat children—or perhaps
it was five. He never could remember the exact number because his memory was so bad.

His Castle was made of silver and granite, and his
coffers were full of gold and the diamonds in his
crown were as big as duck's eggs.

He had many marvellous cities and sailing-ships at
sea. And for his right-hand-man he had a Lord High
Chancellor who knew exactly What was What and
What was Not and advised the King accordingly.

But the King had no wisdom. He was utterly and
absolutely foolish and, what was more, he knew it!

Indeed, he could hardly help knowing it, for everybody, from the Queen and the Lord High Chancellor downwards, was constantly reminding him of the fact. Even bus-conductors and engine-drivers and the people who served in shops could hardly refrain from letting the King know *they* knew he had no wisdom. They didn't dislike him, they merely felt a contempt for him.

It was not the King's fault that he was so stupid. He had tried and tried to learn wisdom ever since he was a boy. But, in the middle of his lessons, even when he was grown up, he would suddenly burst into tears and, wiping his eyes on his ermine train, would cry——

"I know I shall never be any good at it—never! So why nag at me?"

But still his teachers continued to make the effort. Professors came from all over the world to try to teach the King of the Castle something—even if it was only Twice-Times-Two or C-A-T cat. But none of them had the slightest effect on him.

Then the Queen had an idea.

"Let us," she said to the Lord High Chancellor, "offer a reward to the Professor who can teach the King a little wisdom! And if, at the end of a month, he has not succeeded, his head shall be cut off and spiked on the Castle gates as a warning to other Professors of what will happen if they fail."

And, as most of them were rather poor and the reward was a large money-prize, the Professors kept on coming and failing and losing hope, and also their heads. And the spikes of the Castle gates became rather crowded.

Things went from bad to worse. And at last the Queen said to the King——

"Ethelbert," (That was the King's private name) "I really think you had better leave the government of the Kingdom to me and the Lord High Chancellor, as we both know a good deal about everything!"

"But that wouldn't be fair!" said the King, protesting. "After all, it's my Kingdom!"

However he gave in at last because he knew she was cleverer than he. But he so much resented being ordered about in his own Castle and having to use the bent sceptre because he always chewed the knob of the best one, that he went on receiving the Professors and trying to learn wisdom and weeping when he found he couldn't. He wept for their sakes as well as his own for it made him unhappy to see their heads on the gate.

Each new Professor arrived full of hope and assurance and began with some question that the last had not asked.

"What are six and seven, Your Majesty?" enquired a young and handsome Professor who had come from a great distance.

And the King, trying his hardest, thought for a moment. Then he leant forward eagerly and answered——

"Why, twelve, of course!"

"Tch, tch, tch!" said the Lord High Chancellor, standing behind the King's Chair.

The Professor groaned.

"Six and seven are *thirteen*, Your Majesty!"

"Oh, I'm *so* sorry! Try another question, please, Professor! I am sure I shall get the next one right."

"Well, then, what are five and eight?"

"Um—er—let me see! Don't tell me, it's just at the tip of my tongue. Yes! Five and eight are eleven!"

"Tch, tch, tch!" said the Lord High Chancellor.

"THIRTEEN," cried the young Professor hopelessly.

"But, my dear fellow, you just said that six and

seven were thirteen, so how can five and eight be? There aren't two thirteens, surely?"

But the young Professor only shook his head and loosened his collar and went dejectedly away with the Executioner.

"*Is* there more than one thirteen, then?" asked the King nervously.

The Lord High Chancellor turned away in disgust.

"I'm sorry," said the King to himself. "I liked his face so much. It's a pity it has to go on the gate."

And after that he worked very hard at his Arithmetic, hoping that when the next Professor came, he would be able to give the right answers.

He would sit at the top of the Castle steps, just by the draw-bridge, with a book of Multiplication Tables on his knees, saying them over to himself. And while he was looking at the book everything went well but when he shut his eyes and tried to remember them everything went wrong.

"Seven ones are seven, seven twos are thirty-three, seven threes are forty-five—" he began one day. And when he found he was wrong he threw the book away in disgust and buried his head in his cloak.

"It's no good, it's no good! I shall never be wise!" he cried in despair.

Then, because he could not go on weeping for ever, he wiped his eyes and leant back in his golden chair. And as he did that he gave a little start of surprise. For a stranger had pushed past the sentry at the gate and was walking up the path that led to the Castle.

"Hullo," said the King, "who are you?" For he had
no memory for faces.

"Well, if it comes to that," replied the Stranger,
"Who are *you*?"

"I'm the King of the Castle," said the King, picking up the bent sceptre and trying to look important.

"And I'm the Dirty Rascal," was the reply.

The King opened his eyes wide with astonishment.

"Are you really, though? That's interesting! I'm
very pleased to meet you. Do you know seven times
seven?"

"No. Why should I?"

At that the King gave a great cry of delight and,
running down the steps, embraced the Stranger.

"At last, at last!" cried the King, "I have found a
friend. You shall live with me! What is mine shall be
yours! We shall spend our lives together!"

"But, Ethelbert," protested the Queen, "this is
only a Common Person. You cannot have him here."

"Your Majesty," said the Lord High Chancellor,
sternly, "IT WOULD NOT DO."

But for once the King defied him.

"It will do very nicely!" he said royally. "Who is
King here—you or I?"

"Well, of course, in a manner of speaking, *you* are,
as it were, your Majesty, but——"

"Very well. Put this man in cap and bells and he
can be my Fool!"

"Fool!" cried the Queen, wringing her hands. "Do
we need any more of these?"

But the King did not answer. He flung his arm

round the Stranger's neck and the two went dancing
to the Castle door.

"You first!" said the King politely.

"No, you!" said the Stranger.

"Both together, then!" said the King generously,
and they went in side by side.

And from that day the King made no attempt to
learn his lessons. He made a pile of all his books and
burnt them in the courtyard while he and his new
friend danced round it singing—

> "I'm the King of the Castle,
>   And you're the Dirty Rascal!"

"Is that the only song you can sing?" asked the
Fool one day.

"Yes, I'm afraid it is!" said the King, rather sadly.
"Do you know any others?"

"Oh, dear, yes!" said the Fool. And he sang sweetly.

> "Bright, bright
>   Bee in your flight,
>   Drop down some Honey
>   For Supper tonight!"

and

> "Sweet and low, over the Snow,
>   The lolloping, scalloping Lobsters go.
>   Did you know?"

and

> "Boys and Girls, come out to play
>   Over the Hills and Far Away,
>   The Sheep's in the Meadow, the Cow's
>   in the Stall,
>   And down will come Baby, Cradle and All!"

"Lovely!" cried the King, clapping his hands. "Now, listen! I've just thought of one myself! It goes like this—

> "All dogs—Tiddle-de-um!
> Hate frogs—Tiddle-di-do!"

"H'm," said the Fool. "Not bad!"

"Wait a minute!" said the King. "I've thought of another! And I think it's a better one. Listen, carefully!"

And he sang—

> "Pluck me a Flower,
> And catch me a Star,
> And braize them in Butter
> And Treacle and Tar.
>   Tra-la!
> How delicious they are!"

"Bravo!" cried the Fool. "Let's sing it together!"

And he and the King went dancing through the Castle chanting the King's two songs, one after the other, to a very special tune.

And when they were tired of singing they fell together in a heap in the main corridor and there went to sleep.

"He gets worse and worse!" said the Queen to the Lord High Chancellor, "What *are* we to do?"

"I have just heard," replied the Lord High Chancellor, "that the wisest man in the kingdom, the Chief of all the Professors, is coming to-morrow. Perhaps he will help us!"

And the next day the Chief Professor arrived, walk-

"How deep is the sea?"

ing smartly up the path to the Castle carrying a little black bag. It was raining slightly but the whole court had gathered at the top of the steps to welcome him.

"Has he got his wisdom in that little bag, do you think?" whispered the King. But the Fool, who was playing knuckle-bones beside the throne, only smiled and went on tossing.

"Now, if Your Majesty pleases," said the Chief Professor, in a business-like voice, "let us take Arithmetic first. Can Your Majesty answer this? If two Men and a Boy were wheeling a Barrow over a Cloverfield in the middle of February, how many Legs would they have between them?"

The King gazed at him for a moment, rubbing his sceptre against his cheek.

The Fool tossed a knuckle-bone and caught it neatly on the back of his wrist.

"Does it matter?" said the King, smiling pleasantly.

The Chief Professor started violently and looked at the King in astonishment.

"As a matter of fact," he said quietly, "it doesn't. But I will ask your Majesty another question. How deep is the sea?"

"Deep enough to sail a ship on."

Again the Chief Professor stared and his long beard quivered. He was smiling.

"What is the difference, Majesty, between a star and a stone, a bird and a man?"

"No difference at all, Professor. A stone is a star that shines not. A man is a bird without wings."

The Chief Professor drew nearer, and gazed wonderingly at the King.

"What is the best thing in the world?" he asked quietly.

"Doing nothing," answered the King, waving his bent sceptre.

"Oh, dear, oh dear!" wailed the Queen. "THIS IS DREADFUL!"

"Tch! Tch! Tch!" said the Lord High Chancellor.

But the Chief Professor ran up the steps and stood by the King's throne.

"Who taught you these things, Majesty?" he demanded.

The King pointed with his sceptre to the Fool, who was throwing up his knuckle-bones.

"Him," said the King, ungrammatically.

The Chief Professor raised his bushy eyebrows. The Fool looked up at him and smiled. He tossed a knuckle-bone and the Professor, bending forward, caught it on the back of his hand.

"Ha!" he cried. "I know you! Even in that cap and bells, I know the Dirty Rascal!"

"Ha, ha!" laughed the Fool.

"What else did he teach you, Majesty?" The Chief Professor turned again to the King.

"To sing," answered the King.

And he stood up and sang—

> "A black and white Cow
> Sat up in a Tree
> And if I were she
> Then I shouldn't be me!"

"Very true," said the Chief Professor. "What else?"

The King sang again, in a pleasant, quavering voice—

> "The Earth spins round
> Without a tilt
> So that the Sea
> Shall not be spilt."

"So it does," remarked the Chief Professor. "Any more?"

"Oh gracious, yes!" said the King, delighted at his success. "There's this one—

> "Oh, I could learn
> Until I'm pink.
> But then I'd have
> No time to think!"

"Or perhaps, Professor, you'd prefer—

> "We won't go round
> The World for then
> We'd only come
> Back Home again!"

The Chief Professor clapped his hands.

"There's one more," said the King, "if you'd care to hear it."

"Please sing it, Sire!"

And the King cocked his head at the Fool and smiled wickedly and sang—

> "Chief Professors
> All should be
> Drowned in early
> Infancee!"

At the end of the song the Chief Professor gave a loud laugh and fell at the King's feet.

"Oh, King," he said, "live for ever! You have no need of me!"

And without another word he ran down the steps and took off his overcoat, coat and waistcoat. Then he flung himself down upon the grass and called for a plate of Strawberries-and-Cream and a large glass of Beer.

"Tch, tch, tch!" said the horrified Lord High Chancellor. For now all the courtiers were rushing down the steps and taking off their coats and rolling in the rainy grass.

"Strawberries and Beer! Strawberries and Beer!" they shouted thirstily.

"Give him the prize!" said the Chief Professor, sucking his beer through a straw, and nodding in the direction of the Fool.

"Pooh!" said the Fool. "I don't want it. What would I do with it?"

And he scrambled to his feet, put his knuckle-bones in his pocket and strolled off down the path.

"Hi, where are you going?" cried the King anxiously.

"Oh, anywhere, everywhere!" said the Fool airily, sauntering on down the path.

"Wait for me, wait for me!" called the King stumbling over his train as he hurried down the steps.

"Ethelbert! What *are* you doing? You forget yourself!" cried the Queen angrily.

"I do not, my dear!" The King called back. "On the contrary, I am remembering myself for the first time!"

He hurried down the path, caught up with the Fool, and embraced him.

"Ethelbert!" called the Queen again.

The King took no notice.

The rain had ceased but there was still a watery brightness in the air. And presently a rainbow streamed out of the sun and curved in a great arc down to the Castle path.

"I thought we might take this road," said the Fool, pointing.

"What? The rainbow? Is it solid enough? Will it hold us?"

"Try!"

The King looked at the rainbow and its shimmering stripes of violet, blue and green, and yellow and orange and red. Then he looked at the Fool.

"All right, I'm willing!" he said. "Come on!" He stepped up to the coloured path.

"It holds!" cried the King, delightedly. And he ran swiftly up the Rainbow, his train gathered in his hand.

"I'm the King of the Castle!" he sang triumphantly.

"And I'm the Dirty Rascal!" called the Fool, running after him.

"But—it's impossible!" said the Lord High Chancellor, gasping.

The Chief Professor laughed and swallowed another strawberry.

"How can anything that truly happens be impossible?" he enquired.

"But it is! It must be! It's against all the Laws!"

The face of the Lord High Chancellor was purple with anger.

A cry burst from the Queen.

"Oh, Ethelbert, come back!" she implored. "I don't mind how foolish you are if you'll only come back!"

The King glanced down over his shoulder and shook his head. The Fool laughed loudly. Up and up they went together, steadily climbing the rainbow.

Something curved and shining fell at the Queen's feet. It was the bent sceptre. A moment later it was followed by the King's crown.

She stretched out her arms imploringly.

But the King's only answer was a song, sung in his high, quavering voice—

"Say good-bye, Love,
Never cry, Love,
You are wise
And so am I, Love!"

The Fool, with a contemptuous flick of his hand
tossed her down a knuckle-bone. Then he gave the
King a little push, and urged him onwards. The
King picked up his train and ran and the Fool
pounded at his heels. On and on they went up the
bright, coloured path until a cloud passed between
them and the earth and the watching Queen saw
them no longer.

"You are wise,
And so am I, Love!"

The echo of the King's song came floating back. She
heard the last thin thread of it after the King himself
had disappeared.

"Tch, tch, TCH!" said the Lord High Chancellor.
"Such things are simply NOT DONE!"

But the Queen sat down upon the empty throne
and wept.

"Aie!" she cried softly, behind the screen of her
hands. "My King is gone and I am very desolate and
nothing will ever be the same again!"

Meanwhile, the King and the Fool had reached
the top of the rainbow.

"What a climb!" said the King, sitting down and
wrapping his cloak about him. "I think I shall sit
here for a bit—perhaps for a long time. You go on!"

"You won't be lonely?" the Fool enquired.

"Oh, dear, no. Why should I be? It is very quiet

and pleasant up here. And I can always think—or, better still, go to sleep." And as he said that he stretched himself out upon the rainbow with his cloak under his head.

The Fool bent down and kissed him.

"Good-bye, then, King," he said softly. "For you no longer have any need of me."

He left the King quietly sleeping and went whistling down the other side of the rainbow.

And from there he went wandering the world again, as he had done in the days before he met the King, singing and whistling and taking no thought for anything but the immediate moment.

Sometimes he took service with other Kings and high people, and sometimes he went among ordinary men living in small streets or lanes. Sometimes he would be wearing gorgeous livery and sometimes clothes as poor as any one ever stood up in. But no matter where he went he brought good fortune and great luck to the house that roofed him——.

Mary Poppins ceased speaking. For a moment her hands lay still in her lap and her eyes gazed out unseeingly across the Lake.

Then she sighed and gave her shoulders a little shake and stood up.

"Now then!" she said briskly, "Best Feet Forward! And off home!"

She turned to find Jane's eyes fixed steadily upon her.

"You'll know me next time, I hope!" she remarked

tartly. "And you, Michael, get down off that seat at once! Do you want to break your neck and give me the trouble of calling a Policeman?"

She strapped the Twins into the perambulator and pushed it in front of her with a quick impatient movement.

Jane and Michael fell into step behind.

"I wonder where the King of the Castle went when the rainbow disappeared?" said Michael thoughtfully.

"He went with it, I suppose, wherever it goes," said Jane. "But what *I* wonder is—what happened to the Rascal?"

Mary Poppins had wheeled the perambulator into the Elm Walk. And as the children turned the corner, Michael caught Jane's hand.

"There he is!" he cried excitedly, pointing down the Elm Walk to the Park Gates.

A tall slim figure, curiously dressed in red-and-yellow was swaggering towards the entrance. He stood for a moment, looking up and down Cherry Tree Lane, and whistling. Then he slouched across to the opposite pavement and swung himself lazily over one of the garden fences.

"It's ours!" said Jane, recognising it by the brick that had always been missing. "He's gone into our garden. Run, Michael. Let's catch up with him!"

They ran at a gallop after Mary Poppins and the perambulator.

"Now then, now then! No horse-play, please!" said Mary Poppins, grabbing Michael's arm firmly as he rushed by.

"But we want——" he began, squirming.

"*What did I say?*" she demanded, glaring at him so fiercely that he dared not disobey. "Walk beside me, please, like a Christian. And Jane, you can help me push the pram!"

Unwillingly Jane fell into step beside her.

As a rule, Mary Poppins allowed nobody to push the perambulator except herself. But to-day it seemed to Jane that she was purposely preventing them from running ahead. For here was Mary Poppins, who usually walked so quickly that it was difficult to keep up with her, going at a snail's pace down the Elm Walk, pausing every few minutes to gaze about her, and standing for at least a minute in front of a basket of litter.

At last, after what seemed to them like hours, they came to the Park Gates. She kept them beside her until they reached the gate of Number Seventeen. Then they broke from her and went flying through the garden.

They darted behind the lilac tree. Not there! They searched among the rhododendrons and looked in the glasshouse, the tool-shed and the water-butt. They even peered into a circle of hose-piping. The Dirty Rascal was nowhere to be seen!

There was only one other person in the garden and that was Robertson Ay. He was sound asleep in the middle of the lawn with his cheek against the knives of the lawn-mower.

"We've missed him!" said Michael. "He must have taken a short cut and gone out by the back way. Now we'll never see him again."

He turned back to the lawn-mower.

Jane was standing beside it, looking down affectionately at Robertson Ay. His old felt hat was pulled over his face, its crown crushed and dented into a curving peak.

"I wonder if he had a good Half-day!" said Michael, whispering so as not to disturb him.

But, small as the whisper was, Robertson Ay must have heard it. For he suddenly stirred in his sleep and settled himself more comfortably against the lawn-mower. And as he moved there was a faint, jingling sound as though, near at hand, small bells were softly ringing.

With a start, Jane lifted her head and glanced at Michael.

"Did you hear?" she whispered.

He nodded, staring.

Robertson Ay moved again and muttered in his sleep. They bent to listen.

"Black and white cow," he murmured indistinctly. "Sat up in a tree . . . mumble, mumble, mumble . . . it couldn't be me! Hum . . . !"

Across his sleeping body Jane and Michael gazed at each other with wondering eyes.

"Humph! Well to be him, I must say!"

Mary Poppins had come up behind them and she too was staring down at Robertson Ay. "The lazy, idle, Good-for-Nothing!" she said crossly.

But she couldn't really have been as cross as she sounded for she took her handkerchief out of her pocket and slipped it between Robertson Ay's cheek and the lawn-mower.

"He'll have a clean face, anyway, when he wakes up. *That'll* surprise him!" she said tartly.

But Jane and Michael noticed how careful she had been not to wake Robertson Ay and how soft her eyes were when she turned away.

They tip-toed after her, nodding wisely to one another. Each knew that the other understood.

Mary Poppins trundled the perambulator up the steps and into the hall. The front door shut with a quiet little click.

Outside in the garden Robertson Ay slept on.

That night when Jane and Michael went to say good-night to him, Mr. Banks was in a towering rage. He was dressing to go out to dinner and he couldn't find his best stud.

"Well, by all that's lively, here it is!" he cried suddenly. "In a tin of stove-blacking—of all things! on my dressing-table. That Robertson Ay's doing. I'll sack that fellow one of these days. He's nothing but a dirty rascal!"

And he could not understand why Jane and Michael, when he said that, burst into such peals of joyous laughter. . . .

7

THE EVENING OUT

"WHAT, NO PUDDING?" said Michael, as Mary Poppins, her arm full of plates, mugs and knives, began to lay the table for Nursery Tea.

She turned and looked at him fiercely.

"This," she snapped, "is my Evening Out. So you will eat bread and butter and strawberry-jam and be thankful. There's many a little boy would be glad to have it."

"*I'm* not," grumbled Michael. "I want rice-pudding with honey in it."

"You want! You want! You're always wanting. If it's not this it's that, and if it's not that it's the other. You'll ask for the Moon next."

He put his hands in his pockets and moved sulkily away to the window-seat. Jane was kneeling there, staring out at the bright, frosty sky. He climbed up beside her, still looking very cross.

"All right, then! I *do* ask for the Moon. So there!" He flung the words back at Mary Poppins. "But I know I shan't get it. Nobody ever gives me anything."

He turned hurriedly away from her angry glare.

"Jane," he said, "there's no pudding."

"Don't interrupt me, I'm counting!" said Jane,

pressing her nose against the window-pane so that it was quite blunt and squashed at the tip.

"Counting what?" he asked, not very interested. His mind was full of rice-pudding and honey.

"Shooting stars. Look, there goes another. That's seven. And another! Eight. And one over the Park— that's nine!"

"O-o-h! And there's one going down Admiral Boom's chimney!" said Michael, sitting up suddenly and forgetting all about the pudding.

"And a little one—see!—streaking right across the Lane. Such frosty lights!" cried Jane. "Oh, *how* I wish we were out there! What makes stars shoot, Mary Poppins?"

"Do they come out of a gun?" enquired Michael. Mary Poppins sniffed contemptuously.

"What do you think I am? An Encyclopaedia? Everything from A to Z?" she demanded crossly. "Come and eat your teas, please!" She pushed them towards their chairs and pulled down the blind. "And No Nonsense. I'm in a hurry!"

And she made them eat so quickly that they were both afraid they would choke.

"Mayn't I have just *one* more piece?" asked Michael, stretching out his hand to the plate of bread-and-butter.

"You may not. You have already eaten more than is good for you. Take a ginger biscuit and go to bed."

"But——"

"But me no buts or you'll be sorry!" she flung at him sternly.

"I shall have indigestion, I know I shall," he said

to Jane, but only in a whisper, for when Mary Poppins looked like that it was wiser not to make any remark at all. Jane took no notice. She was slowly eating her ginger biscuit and peering cautiously out at the frosty sky through a chink in the blind.

"Thirteen, Fourteen, Fifteen, Sixteen——"

"Did I or did I not say BED?" enquired the familiar voice behind them.

"All right, I'm just going! I'm just going, Mary Poppins!"

And they ran squealing to the Night-nursery with Mary Poppins hurrying after them and looking Simply Awful.

Less than half-an-hour later Mary Poppins was tucking each one in tightly, pushing the sheets and blankets under the mattress with sharp furious little stabs.

"There!" she said, snapping the words between her lips. "That's all for tonight. And if I hear One Word——" She did not finish the sentence but her look said all that was necessary.

"There'll be Trouble!" said Michael, finishing it for her. But he whispered it under his breath to his blanket for he knew what would happen if he said it aloud. She whisked out of the room, her starched apron rustling and crackling, and shut the door with an angry click. They heard her light feet hurrying away down the stairs—Tap-tap, Tap-tap—from landing to landing.

"She's forgotten to light the night-light," said Michael, peering around the corner of his pillow.

"She *must* be in a hurry. I wonder where she's going!"

"And she's left the blind up!" said Jane, sitting up in bed. "Hooray, now we can watch the shooting stars!"

The pointed roofs of Cherry Tree Lane were shiny with frost and the moonlight slid down the gleaming slopes and fell soundlessly into the dark gulfs between the houses. Everything glimmered and shone. The earth was as bright as the sky.

"Seventeen-Eighteen-Nineteen-Twenty——" said Jane, steadily counting as the stars shot down. As fast as one disappeared another came to take its place until it seemed that the whole sky was alive and dancing with the dazzle of shooting stars.

"It's like fireworks," said Michael. "Oh, look at that one! Or the Circus. Do you think they have circuses in Heaven, Jane?"

"I'm not sure!" said Jane doubtfully. "There's the Great Bear and the Little Bear, of course, and Taurus-the-Bull and Leo-the-Lion. But I don't know about a Circus."

"Mary Poppins would know," said Michael, nodding wisely.

"Yes, but she wouldn't tell," said Jane, turning again to the window. "Where was I? Was it Twenty-one? Oh, Michael, *such* a beauty—do you see?" She bounced excitedly up and down in her bed, pointing to the window.

A very bright star, larger than any they had yet seen, was shooting through the sky towards Number Seventeen Cherry Tree Lane. It was different from the others for, instead of leaping straight across the dark, it was turning over and over, curving through the air very curiously.

"Duck your head, Michael!" shouted Jane suddenly. "It's coming in here!"

They dived down into the blankets and burrowed their heads under the pillows.

"Do you think it's gone now?" came Michael's muffled voice presently. "I'm nearly smothercated."

"Of course I haven't gone!" A small clear voice answered him. "What do you take me for?"

Very surprised, Jane and Michael threw off the bed-clothes and sat up. There, at the edge of the window-sill, perched on its shiny tail and gleaming brightly at them, was the shooting star.

"Come on, you two! Be quick!" it said, gleaming frostily across the room.

Michael stared at it.

"But—I don't understand——" he began.

A bright, glittering, very small laugh sounded in the room.

"You never do, do you?" said the star.

"You mean—we're to come with you?" said Jane.

"Of course! And mind you wrap up. It's chilly!"

They sprang out of their beds and ran for overcoats.

"Got any money?" the star asked sharply.

"There's twopence in my coat pocket," said Jane doubtfully.

"Coppers? They'll be no good! Here, catch!" And with a little sizzling sound, as though a firework squib was going off, the star sent out a shower of sparks. Two of them shot right across the room and landed, one in Jane's hand and one in Michael's.

"Hurry, or we'll be late!"

The star streaked across the room, through the closed door and down the stairs with Jane and Michael, tightly clasping their starry money, after it.

"Can I be dreaming I wonder?" said Jane to herself, as she hurried down Cherry Tree Lane.

"Follow!" cried the star as, at the end of the Lane, where the frosty sky seemed to come down to meet the pavement, it leapt into the air and disappeared.

"Follow! Follow!" came the voice from somewhere in the sky. "Just as you are, step on a star!"

Jane seized Michael's hand and raised her foot uncertainly from the pavement. To her surprise she found that the lowest star in the sky was easily within her reach. She stepped up, balancing carefully. The star seemed quite steady and solid.

"Come on, Michael!"

They hurried up the frosty sky, leaping over the gulfs between the stars.

"Follow!" cried the voice, far ahead of them. Jane paused, and glancing down, caught her breath to see how high they were. Cherry Tree Lane—indeed, the whole world—was as small and sparkly as a toy on a Christmas Tree.

"Are you giddy, Michael?" she said, springing on to a large flat star.

"N-o-o. Not if you hold my hand."

They paused. Behind them the great stairway of stars led down to earth but before them there were no more to be seen, nothing but a thick blue patch of naked sky.

Michael's hand trembled in Jane's.

"W-w-what shall we do now?" he said, in a voice that tried not to sound frightened.

"Walk up! Walk up! Walk up and see the sights! Pay your money and take your choice! The two-Tailed Dragon or the Horse with Wings! Magical Marvels! Universal Wonders! Walk up! Walk up!"

A loud voice seemed to be shouting these words in their very ears. They stared about them. There was no sign of anybody.

"Step along everybody! Don't miss the Golden Bull and the Comical Clown! World-Famous Troupe of Performing Constellations! Once seen never forgotten! Push aside the curtain and walk in!"

Again the voice sounded close beside them. Jane put out her hand. To her surprise she found that what had seemed a plain and starless patch of sky was really a thick dark curtain. She pressed against it and felt it yield, she gathered up a fold of it and, pulling Michael after her, pushed the curtain aside.

A bright flare of light dazzled them for a moment. When they could see again they found themselves standing at the edge of a ring of shining sand. The great blue curtain enfolded the ring on all sides and was drawn up to a point above as though it were a tent.

"Now then! Do you know you were almost too late? Got your tickets?"

They turned. Beside them, his bright feet gleaming in the sand, stood a strange and gigantic figure.

He looked like a hunter for a starry leopard-skin was slung across his shoulders and from his belt, decorated with three large stars, hung down a shining sword.

"Tickets, please!" he held out his hand.

"I'm afraid we haven't got any. You see, we didn't know——" began Jane.

"Dear, dear, how careless! Can't let you in without a ticket, you know. But what's that in your hand?"

Jane held out the golden spark.

"Well, if that isn't a ticket, I'd like to know what is!" He pressed the spark between his three large stars. "Another shiner for Orion's belt!" he remarked pleasantly.

"Is that who you are?" said Jane, staring at him.

"Of course—didn't you know? But—excuse me, I must attend to the door. Move along, please!"

The children, feeling rather shy, moved on hand in hand. Tier on tier of seats rose up at one side of them and at the other a golden cord separated them from the ring. And the ring itself was crowded with the strangest collection of animals, all shining bright as gold. A Horse with great gold Wings pranced by on glittering hooves. A golden Fish threshed up the dust of the ring with its fin. Three Little Kids were rushing wildly about on two legs instead of four. And it seemed to Jane and Michael, as they looked closer, that all these animals were made of stars. The wings of the Horse were of stars, not feathers, the Three Kids had stars on their noses and tails and the Fish was covered with shining starry scales.

"Good-evening!" it remarked, bowing politely to

Jane as it threshed by. "Fine night for the performance!"

But before Jane could reply it had hurried past.

"How very strange!" said she. "I've never seen animals like this before!"

"Why should it be strange?" said a voice behind
them.

Two children, both boys and a little older than
Jane, stood there smiling. They were dressed in shining tunics and their peaked caps had each a star for a
pompon.

"I beg your pardon," said Jane, politely. "But, you
see, we're used to—er—fur and feathers and these animals seem to be made of stars."

"But of course they are!" said the first boy, opening his eyes very wide. "What else could they be made
of? They're the Constellations!"

"But even the sawdust is gold——" began Michael.

The second boy laughed. "Star-dust, you mean!
Haven't you been to a Circus before?"

"Not this kind."

"All circuses are alike," said the first boy. "Our
animals are brighter, that's all."

"But who are you?" demanded Michael.

"The Twins. He's Pollux and I'm Castor. We're
always together."

"Like the Siamese Twins?"

"Yes. But more so. The Siamese Twins are only
joined in body but we have a single heart and a single
mind between us. We can think each other's thoughts
and dream each other's dreams. But we mustn't stay
here talking. We've got to get ready—see you later!"

And the Twins ran off and disappeared through a curtained exit.

"Hullo!" said a gloomy voice from inside the ring. "I suppose you don't happen to have a currant bun in your pocket?"

A Dragon with two large finny tails lumbered towards them, breathing steam from its nostrils.

"I'm sorry, we haven't," said Jane.

"Nor a biscuit or two?" said the Dragon eagerly.

They shook their heads.

"I thought not," said the Dragon, dropping a golden tear. "It's always the way on Circus nights. I don't get fed till after the performance. On ordinary occasions I have a beautiful maiden for supper——"

Jane drew back quickly, pulling Michael with her.

"Oh, don't be alarmed!" the Dragon went on, reassuringly. "You'd be *much* too small. Besides, you're human and therefore tasteless. They keep me hungry," he explained, "so that I shall do my tricks better. But after the show——" A greedy light came into his eyes and he shuffled away, lolling out his tongue and saying "Yum-yum" in a soft, greedy, hissing voice.

"I'm glad we're only human," said Jane, turning to Michael. "It would be *dreadful* to be eaten by a Dragon!"

But Michael had hurried on ahead and was talking eagerly to the Three Little Kids.

"How does it go?" he was asking, as Jane caught up with him.

And the Eldest Kid, which apparently had offered to recite, cleared its throat, and began—

"Horn and toe,
Toe and horn——"

"Now, Kids!" Orion's voice interrupted loudly.
"You can say your piece when the time comes. Get
ready now, we're going to begin! Follow me, please!"
he said to the children.

They trotted obediently after the gleaming figure
and as they went the golden animals turned to stare
at them. They heard snatches of whispered conversation as they passed.

"Who's that?" said a huge starry Bull, as it stopped
pawing the star-dust to gaze at them. And a Lion
turned and whispered something into the Bull's ear.
They caught the words "Banks" and "Evening Out"
but heard no more than that.

By now every seat on every tier was filled with a
shining starry figure. Only three empty seats
remained and to these Orion led the children.

"Here you are! We kept these for you. Just under
the Royal Box. You'll see perfectly. Look! they're just
beginning!"

And, turning, Jane and Michael saw that the ring
was empty. The animals had hurried out while they
had been climbing to their seats. They unbuttoned
their overcoats and leaned forward excitedly.

From somewhere came a fanfare of trumpets. A
blast of music echoed through the tent and above the
sound could be heard a high, sweet neighing.

"The comets!" said Orion, sitting down beside
Michael.

A wild nodding head appeared at the entrance and

one by one nine comets galloped into the ring, their manes braided with gold, and silver plumes on their heads.

Suddenly the music rose to a great roar of sound and with one movement the comets dropped upon their knees and bowed their heads. A warm gust of air came wafting across the ring.

"How hot it's getting!" cried Jane.

"Hush! He's coming!" said Orion.

"Who?" whispered Michael.

"The Ring-Master!"

Orion nodded to the far entrance. A light shone there eclipsing the light of the constellations. It grew steadily brighter.

"Here he is!" Orion's voice had a curious softness in it.

And as he spoke there appeared between the curtains a towering golden figure with flaming curls upon his head and a wide, radiant face. And with him came a great swell of warmth that lapped the ring and spread out in ever-widening circles until it surrounded Jane and Michael and Orion. Half-consciously, made dreamy by that warmth, the children slipped off their overcoats.

Orion sprang to his feet holding his right hand above his head.

"Hail, Sun, hail!" he cried. And from the stars in the tiered seats the cry came echoing——

"Hail!"

The Sun glanced round the wide dark-tented ring and, in answer to the greeting, swung his long gold whip three times about his head. As the lash turned in the air there was a quick, sharp crack. At once the comets sprang up and cantered out, their braided tails swinging wildly, their plumed heads high and erect.

"Here we are again, here we are again!" cried a loud, hoarse voice, and bouncing into the ring came a comical figure with silver-painted face, wide red mouth and huge silvery frills about his neck.

"Saturn—the Clown!" whispered Orion behind his hand to the children.

"When is a door not a door?" demanded the Clown of the audience, turning over and standing on one hand.

"When it's ajar!" answered Jane and Michael loudly.

A disappointed look came over the Clown's face.

"Oh, you know it!" he said, reproachfully. "That's not fair!"

The Sun cracked his whip.

"All right, all right!" said the Clown. "I've got another. Why does a hen cross the road?" he asked, sitting down with a bump on the star-dust.

"To get to the other side!" cried Jane and Michael. The swinging whip caught the Clown round the knees.

"O-o-h! Don't do that! You'll hurt poor Joey. Look at them laughing up there! But I'll fix them! Listen!" He turned a double somersault in the air.

"What kind of jam did the chicken ask for when it came out of the egg. Tell me that!"

"Mar—me—lade!" yelled Michael and Jane.

"Be off with you!" cried the Sun, catching his whip about the Clown's shoulders, and the Clown went bounding round the ring, head over heels, crying——

"Poor old Joey! He's failed again! They know all

his best jokes, poor old fellow, poor old—oh, beg pardon, Miss, beg pardon!"

He broke off for he had somersaulted against Pegasus, the Winged Horse, as it entered carrying a bright spangly figure on its back.

"Venus, the Evening Star," explained Orion.

Breathlessly, Jane and Michael watched the starry figure ride lightly through the ring. Round and round she went, bowing to the Sun as she passed and presently the Sun, standing in her path, held up a great hoop covered with thin gold paper.

She balanced on her toes for a moment. "Hup!" said the Sun, and Venus with the utmost grace, jumped through the hoop and landed again on the back of Pegasus.

"Hurrah!" cried Jane and Michael, and the audience of stars echoed back "Hurrah!"

"Let me try, let Poor Joey have a go, just a little one to make a cat laugh!" cried the Clown. But Venus only tossed her head and laughed and rode out of the ring.

She had hardly disappeared before the Three Kids came prancing in, looking rather shy, and bowing awkwardly to the Sun. Then they stood on their hind-legs in a row before him, and in high, thin voices recited the following song—

> "Horn and hoof,
> Hoof and horn,
> Every night
> Three Kids are born,
> Each with a Twinkly Nose,
> Each with a Twinkly Tail.

Blue and black,
Black and blue
Is the evening sky
As the Kids come through,
Each with a Twinkly Nose,
Each with a Twinkly Tail.

Gay and bright
And white as May
The Three Kids drink
At the Milky Way,
Each with a Twinkly Nose,
Each with a Twinkly Tail.

> All night long
> From Dusk till Dawn
> The Three Kids graze
> On the starry lawn
> Each with a Twinkly Nose,
> Each with a Twink-ker-ly T-a-i-ll"

They drew out the last line with a long baa-ing sound and danced out.

"What's next?" asked Michael but there was no need for Orion to reply for the Dragon was already in the ring, his nostrils steaming and his two finny tails tossing up the star-dust. After him came Castor and Pollux carrying between them a large white shining globe faintly figured with a design of mountains and rivers.

"It looks like the Moon!" said Jane.

"Of course it's the Moon!" said Orion.

The Dragon was now on his hind legs and the Twins were balancing the Moon on his nose. It bobbed up and down uncertainly for a moment. Then it settled and the Dragon began to waltz about the ring to the tune of the starry music. Round he went, very carefully and steadily, once, twice, three times.

"That will do!" said the Sun cracking his whip. And the Dragon, with a sigh of relief, shook its head and sent the Moon flying across the ring. It landed, with a bumpy thud, right in Michael's lap.

"Good gracious!" said he, very startled. "What shall I do with this?"

"Whatever you like," said Orion. "I thought you asked for it."

And suddenly Michael remembered his conversation that evening with Mary Poppins. He had asked for the Moon then and now he had got it. And he didn't know what to do with it. How very awkward!

But he had no time to worry about it for the Sun was cracking his whip again. Michael settled the Moon on his knee, folded his arms around it and turned back to the ring.

"What are two and three?" the Sun was asking the Dragon.

The two tails lashed five times on the star-dust.

"And six and four?" The Dragon thought for a minute. One, two, three, four, five, six, seven, eight, nine—— The tails stopped.

"Wrong!" said the Sun. "Quite wrong! No supper for you to-night!"

At that the Dragon burst into tears and hurried from the ring sobbing.

"Alas and alack,
   Boo-hoo, boo-hoo!"

he cried bitterly.

"I wanted a Maiden
   Served in a stew,
   A succulent, seasoned, tasty Girl
   With star for her eye
   And comet for curl,
   And I wouldn't have minded if there'd been two,
   For I'm awfully hungry.
                            Boo-hoo!
                                    Boo-hoo!"

"Won't they give him even a small maiden?" said
Michael, feeling rather sorry for the Dragon.

"Hush!" said Orion, as a dazzling form sprang into
the ring.

When the cloud of star-dust had cleared away, the
children drew back, startled. It was the Lion and he
was growling fiercely.

Michael moved a little closer to Jane.

The Lion, crouching, moved forward slowly till he
reached the Sun. His long red tongue went out, lolling dangerously. But the Sun only laughed, and lifting his foot, he gently kicked the Lion's golden nose.
With a roar, as though he had been burnt, the starry
beast sprang up.

The Sun's whip cracked fiercely on the air. Slowly,
unwillingly, growling all the time, the Lion rose on
his hind legs. The Sun tossed him a skipping-rope
and, holding it between his forepaws, the lion began
to sing.

"I am the Lion, Leo-the-Lion,
The beautiful, suitable, Dandy Lion,
Look for me up in the starry sky on
Clear cold nights at the foot of Orion,
Glimmering, glittering, gleaming there,
The Handsomest Sight in the atmosphere!"

And at the end of the song he swung the rope and skipped round the ring, rolling his eyes and growling.

"Hurry up, Leo, it's our turn!" A rumbling voice sounded from behind the curtain.

"Come on, you big cat!" a shrill voice added.

The Lion dropped his skipping-rope and with a roar sprang at the curtain, but the two creatures who entered next stepped carefully aside so that the Lion missed them.

"Great Bear and Little Bear," said Orion.

Slowly the two Bears lumbered in, holding paws and waltzing to slow music. Round the ring they went, looking very serious and solemn, and at the end of their dance they made a clumsy curtsey to the audiance and remarked—

"We're the Gruffly Bear and the Squeaky Bear,
O Constellations, has any one here
A honeycomb square that they can spare
For the Squeaky Bear and the Gruffly Bear
To add to the store in their dark blue lair
Or to——
          or to——
                  or to——"

The Great Bear and the Little Bear stammered and stumbled and looked at each other.

"Don't you remember what comes next?" rumbled the Gruffly Bear behind his paw.

"No, I don't!" The Squeaky Bear shook his head and stared anxiously down at the star-dust as though he thought the missing words might be there.

But at that moment the audience saved the situation. A shower of honeycombs came hurtling down, tumbling about the ears of the two Bears. The Gruffly Bear and the Squeaky Bear, looking very relieved, stooped and picked them up.

"Good!" rumbled the Great Bear, digging his nose into a comb.

"*Ex*-cellent!" squeaked the Little Bear trying another. Then, with their noses streaming with honey, they bowed solemnly to the Sun and lumbered out.

The Sun waved his hand and the music grew louder and rang triumphantly through the tent.

"The signal for the Big Parade," said Orion, as Castor and Pollux came dancing in with all the constellations at their heels.

The Bears came back, waltzing clumsily together, and Leo-the-Lion, still growling angrily, came sniffing at their heels. In swept a starry Swan, singing a high, clear chant.

"The Swan Song," said Orion.

And after the Swan came the Golden Fish, leading the Three Kids by a silver string, and the Dragon followed, still sobbing bitterly. A loud and terrible sound almost drowned the music. It was the bellowing of Taurus-the-Bull as he leapt into the ring, trying to toss Saturn the Clown from his back. One after another the creatures came rushing in to take their places. The ring was a swaying golden mass of horns and hooves and manes and tails.

"Is this the end?" Jane whispered.

"Almost," replied Orion. "They're finishing early to-night. She has to be in by half-past ten."

"Who has?" asked both the children together. But Orion did not hear. He was standing up in his seat waving his arm.

"Come along, be quick there, step along!" he called.

And in came Venus riding her Winged Horse followed by a starry Serpent that put its tail carefully in its mouth and bowled along like a hoop.

Last of all came the comets, prancing proudly through the curtains, swinging their braided tails. The music was louder now and wilder and a golden smoke rose up from the star-dust as the constellations, shouting, singing, roaring, growling, formed themselves into a ring. And in the centre, as though they dared not go too near his presence, they left a clear, bare circle for the Sun.

There he stood, towering above them all, his whip folded in his arms. He nodded lightly to each animal as it passed him with bent head. And then Jane and Michael saw that bright gaze lift from the ring and wander round the great audience of watching stars until it turned in the direction of the Royal Box. They felt themselves growing warmer as his rays fell upon them and, with a start of surprise, they saw him raise his whip and nod his head towards them.

As the lash swung up every star and constellation

turned in its tracks. Then, with one movement, every one of them bowed.

"Are they—can they be bowing to *us*?" whispered Michael, clutching the Moon more tightly.

A familiar laugh sounded behind them. They turned quickly. There, sitting alone in the Royal Box, sat a well-known figure in a straw hat and blue coat and a gold locket round its neck.

"Hail, Mary Poppins, hail!" came the massed voices from the circus ring.

Jane and Michael looked at each other. So this was what Mary Poppins did on her Evening Out! They could hardly believe their eyes—and yet, there *was* Mary Poppins, as large as life and looking very superior.

"Hail!" came the cry again.

Mary Poppins raised her hand in greeting.

Then, stepping primly and importantly, she moved out of the box. She did not seem in the least surprised to see Jane and Michael but she sniffed as she went past.

"How often," she remarked to them across Orion's head, "have you been told that it is rude to stare?"

She passed on and down to the ring. The Great Bear lifted the golden rope. The Constellations drew apart and the Sun moved a pace forward. He spoke and his voice was warm and full of sweetness.

"Mary Poppins, my dear, you are welcome!"

Mary Poppins dropped to her knees in a deep curtsey.

"The Planets hail you and the Constellations give you greeting. Rise, my child!"

"How often," she remarked, *"have you been told that it is rude to stare?"*

She stood up, bending her head respectfully before him.

"For you, Mary Poppins," the Sun went on, "the Stars have gathered in the dark blue tent, for you they have been withdrawn to-night from shining on the world. I trust, therefore, that you have enjoyed your Evening Out!"

"I never had a better one. Never!" said Mary Poppins, lifting her head and smiling.

"Dear child!" The Sun bowed. "But now the sands of night are running out, and you must be in by half-past-ten. So, before you depart, let us all, for old sake's sake, dance the Dance of the Wheeling Sky!"

"Down you go!" said Orion, to the astonished children, giving them a little push. They stumbled down the stairs and almost fell into the star-dust ring.

"And where, may I ask, are your manners?" hissed the well-known voice in Jane's ear.

"What must I do?" stammered Jane.

Mary Poppins glared at her and made a little movement towards the Sun. And, suddenly, Jane realized. She grabbed Michael's arm, and, kneeling, pulled him down beside her. The warmth from the Sun lapped them about with fiery sweetness.

"Rise, children," he said kindly. "You are very welcome. I know you well—I have looked down upon you many a summer's day!"

Scrambling to her feet Jane moved towards him but his whip held her back. "Touch me not, child of earth!" he cried warningly, waving her further away. "Life is sweet and no man may come near the Sun—touch me not!"

"But are you truly the Sun?" demanded Michael, staring at him.

The Sun flung out his hand.

"O Stars and Constellations," he said, "tell me this. Who am I? This child would know?"

"Lord of the Stars, O Sun!" answered a thousand starry voices.

"He is King of the South and North," cried Orion, "and Ruler of the East and West. He walks the outer rim of the world and the Poles melt in his glory. He draws up the leaf from the seed and covers the land with sweetness. He is truly the Sun."

The Sun smiled across at Michael.

"Now do you believe?"

Michael nodded.

"Then, strike up! And you, Constellations, choose your Partners!"

The Sun waved his whip. The music began again, very swift and gay and dancey. Michael began to beat time with his feet as he hugged the Moon in his arms. But he squeezed it a little too tightly for suddenly there was a loud pop and the Moon began to dwindle.

"Oh! Oh! Look what's happening!" cried Michael, almost weeping.

Down, down, down, shrank the Moon until it was as small as a soap-bubble, then it was only a wisp of shining light and then—his hands closed upon empty air.

"It couldn't have been a real Moon, could it?" he demanded.

Jane glanced questioningly at the Sun across the little stretch of star-dust.

He flung back his flaming head and smiled at her.

"What is real and what is not? Can you tell me or I you? Perhaps we shall never know more than this—that to think a thing is to make it true. And so, if Michael thought he had the Moon in his arms—why, then, he had indeed."

"Then," said Jane wonderingly, "is it true that we are here to-night or do we only think we are?"

The Sun smiled again, a little sadly.

"Child," he said, "seek no further! From the beginning of the world all men have asked that question. And I, who am Lord of the Sky—even I do not know the answer. I am certain only that this is the Evening Out, that the Constellations are shining in your eyes and that it is true if you think it is. . . ."

"Come, dance with us, Jane and Michael!" cried the Twins.

And Jane forgot her question as the four of them swung out into the ring in time with the heavenly tune. But they were hardly half-way round the ring before, with a little start, she stumbled and stood still.

"Look! Look! She is dancing with him!"

Michael followed her gaze and stood still on his short fat legs, staring.

Mary Poppins and the Sun were dancing together. But not as Jane and he were dancing with the Twins, breast to breast and foot to foot. Mary Poppins and the Sun never once touched, but waltzed with arms outstretched, opposite each other, keeping perfect time together in spite of the space between them.

About them wheeled the dancing constellations, Venus with her arms round the neck of Pegasus, the

Bull and the Lion arm in arm and the Three Kids prancing in a row. Their moving brightness dazzled the children's eyes as they stood in the star-dust gazing.

Then suddenly the dance slackened and the music died away. The Sun and Mary Poppins, together yet apart, stood still. And at the same time every animal paused in the dance and stood quietly in its tracks. The whole ring was silent.

The Sun spoke.

"Now," he said quietly, "the time has come. Back to your places in the sky, my stars and constellations. Home and to sleep, my three dear mortal guests. Mary Poppins, good-night! I do not say good-bye for we shall meet again. But—for a little time—farewell, farewell!"

Then, with a large and gracious movement of his head, the Sun leaned across the space that separated him from Mary Poppins and, with great ceremony, carefully, lightly, swiftly, he brushed her cheek with his lips.

"Ah!" cried the Constellations, enviously, "The Kiss! The Kiss!"

But as she received it, Mary Poppins' hand flew to her cheek protectingly, as though the kiss had burnt it. A look of pain crossed her face for a moment. Then, with a smile, she lifted her head to the Sun.

"Farewell!" she said softly, in a voice Jane and Michael had never heard her use.

"Away!" cried the Sun, stretching out his whip. And obediently the Constellations began to rush from the ring. Castor and Pollux joined arms protectingly about the children, that the Great Bear might not brush them as he lumbered by, nor the Bull's horns graze them, nor the Lion do them harm. But in Jane's ears and Michael's the sounds of the ring were growing fainter. Their heads fell sideways, dropping heavily upon their shoulders. Other arms came round them and, as in a dream, they heard the voice of Venus saying—"Give them to me! I am the Homeward Star. I bring the lamb to the fold and the child to its Mother."

They gave themselves up to her rocking arms, swinging lightly with her as a boat swings with the tide.

To and fro, to and fro.

A light flickered across their eyes. Was that the Dragon going brightly by or the nursery candle held guttering above them?

To and fro, to and fro.

They nestled down into soft, sweet warmth. Was it the lapping heat of the Sun? Or the eiderdown on a nursery bed?

"I think it is the Sun," thought Jane, dreamily.

"I think it is my eiderdown," thought Michael.

And a far-away voice, like a dream, like a breath, cried faintly, faintly—"It is whatever you think it is. Farewell. . . . Farewell. . . ."

Michael woke with a shout. He had suddenly remembered something.

"My overcoat! My overcoat! I left it under the Royal Box!"

He opened his eyes. He saw the painted duck at the end of his bed. He saw the mantel-piece with the clock and the Royal Doulton Bowl and the jam-jar full of green leaves. And he saw, hanging on its usual hook, his overcoat with his hat just above it.

"But where are the stars?" he called, sitting up in bed and staring. "I want the stars and Constellations!"

"Oh? Indeed?" said Mary Poppins, coming into the room and looking very stiff and starched in her clean apron. "Is that all? I wonder you don't ask for the Moon, too!"

"But I did!" he reminded her reproachfully. "And I got it, too! But I squeezed it too tight and it bust!"

"Burst!"

"Well, burst, then!"

"Stuff!" said Mary Poppins, tossing him his dressing-gown.

"Is it morning already?" said Jane, opening her

eyes and gazing round the room very surprised to find herself in her own bed. "But how did we get back? I was dancing with the Twin stars, Castor and Pollux."

"You two and your stars," said Mary Poppins crossly, pulling back the blankets. "I'll star you. Spit-spot out of bed, please. I'm late already."

"I suppose you danced too long last night," said Michael, bundling unwillingly out on to the floor.

"Danced? Humph, a lot of dancing I get a chance for, don't I—looking after the five worst children in the world!"

Mary Poppins sniffed and looked very sorry for herself and as if she had not had enough sleep.

"But weren't you dancing—on your Evening Out?" said Jane. For she was remembering how Mary Poppins and the Sun had waltzed together in the centre of the star-dust ring.

Mary Poppins opened her eyes wide.

"I hope," she remarked, drawing herself up haughtily, "I have something better to do with my Evening Out than to go round and round like a Careering Whirligig."

"But I saw you!" said Jane. "Up in the sky. You jumped down from the Royal Box and went to dance in the ring."

Holding their breaths, she and Michael gazed at Mary Poppins as her face slowly flushed red with fury.

"You," she said shortly, "have been having a nice sort of a nightmare, I must say. Who ever heard of me, a person in my position, jumping down from——"

"But I had the nightmare, too," interrupted Michael, "and it was lovely. I was in the sky with Jane and I *saw* you!"

"What, jumping?"

"Er—yes—and dancing."

"In the sky?" He trembled as she came towards him. Her face was dark and terrible.

"One more insult——" she said threateningly, "Just *one more* and you'll find yourself dancing in the corner. So I warn you!"

He hurriedly looked the other way, tying the cord of his dressing-gown and Mary Poppins, her very apron crackling with anger, flounced across the room to wake up the Twins.

Jane sat on her bed staring at Mary Poppins as she bent over the cots.

Michael slowly put on his slippers and sighed.

"We *must* have dreamt it after all," he said sadly. "I wish it had been true."

"It *was* true," said Jane in a cautious whisper, her eyes still fixed on Mary Poppins.

"How do you know? Are you sure?"

"Quite sure. Look!"

Mary Poppins' head was bent over Barbara's cot. Jane nodded towards it. "Look at her face," she whispered in his ear.

Michael regarded Mary Poppins' face steadily. There was the black hair looped back behind the ears, there the familiar blue eyes so like a Dutch doll's, and there were the turned-up nose and the bright red shiny cheeks.

"I can't see anything——" he began and broke off

suddenly. For now, as Mary Poppins turned her head, he saw what Jane had seen.

Burning bright, in the very centre of her cheek, was a small fiery mark. And, looking closer, Michael saw that it was curiously shaped. It was round, with curly, flame-shaped edges and like a very small sun.

"You see?" said Jane softly. "That's where he kissed her."

Michael nodded—one, twice, three times.

"Yes," he said, standing very still and staring at Mary Poppins. "I do see. I do. . . ."

8

BALLOONS *AND* BALLOONS

"I WONDER, Mary Poppins," said Mrs. Banks, hurrying into the Nursery one morning, "if you will have time to do some shopping for me?"

And she gave Mary Poppins a sweet, nervous smile as though she were uncertain what the answer would be.

Mary Poppins turned from the fire where she was airing Annabel's clothes.

"I might," she remarked, not very encouragingly.

"Oh, I see——" said Mrs. Banks and she looked more nervous than ever.

"Or again—I might not," continued Mary Poppins, busily shaking out a woollen jacket and hanging it over the fire-guard.

"Well—in case you *did* have time, here is the List and here is a Pound Note. And if there is any change left over you may spend it!"

Mrs. Banks put the money on the chest of drawers.

Mary Poppins said nothing. She just sniffed.

"Oh!" said Mrs. Banks, suddenly remembering something. "And the Twins must walk to-day, Mary Poppins. Robertson Ay sat down on the perambulator this morning. He mistook it for an arm-chair.

So it will have to be mended. Can you manage without it—and carry Annabel?"

Mary Poppins opened her mouth and closed it again with a snap.

"I," she remarked tartly, "can manage anything—and more, if I choose."

"I—I know!" said Mrs. Banks, edging towards the door. "You are a Treasure—a perfect Treasure—an absolutely wonderful and altogether suitable Treas——" Her voice died away as she hurried down the stairs.

"And yet—and yet—I sometimes wish she wasn't!" Mrs. Banks remarked to her great-grandmother's portrait as she dusted the Drawing-room. "She makes me feel small and silly, as though I were a little girl again. And I'm not!" Mrs. Banks tossed her head and flicked a speck of dust from the spotted cow on the mantelpiece. "I'm a very important person and the Mother of five children. She forgets that!" And she went on with her work thinking out all the things she would like to say to Mary Poppins but knowing all the time that she would never dare.

Mary Poppins put the list and the Pound Note into her bag and in no time she had pinned on her hat and was hurrying out of the house with Annabel in her arms and Jane and Michael, each holding the hand of a Twin, following as quickly as they could.

"Best foot forward, please!" she remarked, turning sternly upon them.

They quickened their pace, dragging the poor Twins with a shuffling sound along the pavement. They forgot that John's arm and Barbara's were being

pulled nearly out of their sockets. Their only thought
was to keep up with Mary Poppins and see what she
did with the change from the Pound Note.

"Two packets of candles, four pounds of rice, three
of brown sugar and six of castor; two tins of tomato
soup and a hearth-brush, a pair of house-maid's
gloves, half-a-stick of sealing-wax, one bag of flour, one
fire-lighter, two boxes of matches, two cauliflowers
and a bundle of rhubarb!"

Mary Poppins, hurrying into the first shop beyond
the Park, read out the list.

The Grocer, who was fat and bald and rather short
of breath, took down the order as quickly as he could.

"One bag of housemaid's gloves——" he wrote, nervously licking the wrong end of his blunt little pencil.

"Flour, I said!" Mary Poppins reminded him tartly.

The Grocer blushed as red as a mulberry.

"Oh, I'm sorry. No offense meant, I'm sure. Lovely
day, isn't it? Yes. My mistake. One bag of house—er—
flour."

He hurriedly scribbled it down and added——

"Two boxes of hearth-brushes——"

"Matches!" snapped Mary Poppins.

The Grocer's hands trembled on his pad.

"Oh, of course. It must be the pencil—it seems to
write all the wrong things. I must get a new one.
Matches, of course! And then you said——?" He
looked up nervously and then down again at his little
stub of pencil.

Mary Poppins, unfolded the list, read it out again
in an angry, impatient voice.

"Sorry," said the Grocer, as she came to the end. "But rhubarb's off. Would damsons do?"

"Certainly not. A packet of tapioca."

"Oh, no, Mary Poppins—not Tapioca. We had that last week," Michael reminded her.

She glanced at him and then at the Grocer and by the look in her eye they both knew that there was no hope. Tapioca it would be. The Grocer, blushing redder than ever, went away to get it.

"There won't be any change left if she goes on like this," said Jane, watching the pile of groceries being heaped upon the counter.

"She might have enough left over for a bag of acid-drops—but that's all," Michael said mournfully, as Mary Poppins took the Pound Note out of her bag.

"Thank you," she said, as the Grocer handed her the change.

"Thank *you*!" he remarked politely, leaning his arms on the counter. He smiled at her in a manner that was meant to be pleasant and continued, "Keeps nice and fine, doesn't it?" He spoke proudly as though he, himself, had complete charge of the weather and had made it fine for her on purpose.

"We want rain!" said Mary Poppins, snapping her mouth and her hand-bag at the same time.

"That's right," said the Grocer hurriedly, trying not to offend her. "Rain's always pleasant."

"Never!" retorted Mary Poppins, tossing Annabel into a more comfortable position on her arm.

The Grocer's face fell. *Nothing* he said was right.

"I hope," he remarked, opening the door courte-

ously for Mary Poppins, "that we shall be favoured
with your further custom, Madam."

"Good-day!" Mary Poppins swept out.

The Grocer sighed.

"Here," he said, scrabbling hurriedly in a box near
the door. "Take these. I meant no harm, truly I
didn't. I only wanted to oblige."

Jane and Michael held out their hands. The Grocer slipped three chocolate drops into Michael's and
two into Jane's.

"One for each of you, one for the two little ones
and one for——" he nodded towards Mary Poppins
retreating figure—"her!"

They thanked the Grocer and hurried after Mary
Poppins, munching their chocolate drops.

"What's that you're eating?" she demanded, looking at the dark rim round Michael's mouth.

"Chocolates. The Grocer gave us one each. And
one for you." He held out the last drop. It was very
sticky.

"Like his impudence!" said Mary Poppins, but she
took the chocolate drop and ate it in two bites as
though she thoroughly enjoyed it.

"Is there much change left?" enquired Michael
anxiously.

"That's as may be."

She swept into the Chemist's and came out with a
cake of soap, a mustard plaster and a tube of tooth-
paste.

Jane and Michael, waiting with the Twins at the
door, sighed heavily.

The Pound Note, they knew, was disappearing fast.

"She'll hardly have enough left over for a stamp and, even if she has, *that* won't be very interesting," said Jane.

"Now to Mr. Tip's!" snapped Mary Poppins, swinging the Chemist's packages and her bag from one hand and holding Annabel tightly with the other.

"But what can we buy *there*?" said Michael in despair. For there was not much jingle in Mary Poppins' purse.

"Coal—two tons and a half," she said, hurrying ahead.

"How much is coal?"

"Two pounds a ton."

"But—Mary Poppins! We can't buy *that*!" Michael stared at her, appalled.

"It will go on the bill."

This was such a relief to Jane and Michael that they bounded beside her, dragging John and Barbara behind them at a trot.

"Well, is that all?" Michael asked, when Mr. Tip and his coals had been left safely behind.

"Cake shop!" said Mary Poppins, examining her list and darting in at a dark door. Through the window they could see her pointing to a pile of macaroons. The assistant handed her a large bag.

"She's bought a dozen at least," said Jane sadly. Usually the sight of anybody buying a macaroon filled them with delight, but to-day they wished and wished that there wasn't a macaroon in the world.

"*Now* where?" demanded Michael, hopping from one leg to the other in his anxiety to know if there were any of the Pound Note left. He felt sure there couldn't be and yet—he hoped.

"Home," said Mary Poppins.

Their faces fell. There was no change, after all, not even a penny or Mary Poppins would surely have spent it. But Mary Poppins, as she dumped the bag of macaroons up on Annabel's chest and strode ahead, had such a look on her face that they did not dare to make any remark. They only knew that, for once, she had disappointed them and they felt they could not forgive her.

"But—this isn't the way home," complained Michael, dragging his feet so that his toes scraped along the pavement.

"Isn't the Park on the way home, I'd like to know?" she demanded, turning fiercely upon him.

"Yes—but——"

"There are more ways than one of going through a Park," she remarked and led them round to a side of it they had never seen before.

The sun shone warmly down. The tall trees bowed over the railings and rustled their leaves. Up in the branches two sparrows were fighting over a piece of straw. A squirrel hopped along the stone balustrade and sat up on his hindquarters, asking for nuts.

But to-day these things did not matter. Jane and Michael were not interested. All they could think of was the fact that Mary Poppins had spent the whole Pound Note on unimportant things and had kept nothing over.

Tired and disappointed, they trailed after her towards the Gates.

Over the entrance, a new one they had never seen before, spread a tall stone arch, splendidly carved with a Lion and a Unicorn. And beneath the arch sat an old, old woman, her face as grey as the stone

itself and as withered and wrinkled as a walnut. On her little old knees she held a tray piled up with what looked like small coloured strips of rubber and above her head, tied firmly to the Park railings, a cluster of bright balloons bobbed and bounced and bounded.

"Balloons! Balloons!" shouted Jane. And, loosening her hand from John's sticky fingers, she ran towards the old woman. Michael bounded after her, leaving Barbara alone and lost in the middle of the pavement.

"Well, my deary ducks!" said the Balloon Woman in an old cracked voice. "Which will you have? Take your choice! And take your time!" She leant forward and shook her tray in front of them.

"We only came to look," Jane explained. "We've got no money."

"Tch, tch, tch! What's the good of *looking* at a balloon? You've got to feel a balloon, you've got to hold a balloon, you've got to *know* a balloon! Coming to look! What good will that do you?"

The old woman's voice crackled like a little flame. She rocked herself on her stool.

Jane and Michael stared at her helplessly. They knew she was speaking the truth. But what could they do?

"When I was a girl," the old woman went on, "people really *understood* balloons. They didn't just come and look! They took—yes, they *took*! There wasn't a child that went through these gates without one. They wouldn't have insulted the Balloon Woman in those days by just looking and passing by!"

She bent her head back and gazed up at the bouncing balloons above her.

"Ah, my loves and doves!" she cried. "They don't understand you any more—nobody but the old woman understands. You're old-fashioned now. Nobody wants you!"

"We *do* want one," said Michael stoutly. "But we

haven't any money. *She* spent the whole Pound Note
on——"

"And who is 'she'?" enquired a voice close behind
him.

He turned and his face went pink.

"I meant—er—that you—er——" he began nervously.

"Speak politely of your betters!" remarked Mary
Poppins and, stretching her arm over his shoulder,
she put half-a-crown on the Balloon Woman's tray.

Michael stared at it, shining there among the limp
un-blown balloons.

"Then there was some change over!" said Jane,
wishing she had not thought so crossly of Mary Poppins.

The Balloon Woman, her old eyes sparkling, picked
up the coin, and gazed at it for a long moment.

"Shiny, shiny, King-and-Crown!" she cried. "I
haven't seen one of these since I was a girl." She
cocked her head at Mary Poppins. "Do you want a
balloon, my lass?"

"*If* you please!" said Mary Poppins with haughty
politeness.

"How many, my deary-duck, how many?"

"Four!"

Jane and Michael, almost jumping out of their
skins, turned and flung their arms round her.

"Oh, Mary Poppins, do you mean it? One each?
Really-really?"

"I hope I always say what I mean," she said primly,
looking very conceited.

They sprang towards the tray and began to turn
over the coloured balloon-cases.

The Balloon Woman slipped the silver coin into a pocket in her skirt. "There, my shiny!" she said, giving the pocket a loving pat. Then, with excited trembling hands, she helped the children turn over the cases.

"Go carefully, my deary-ducks!" she warned them. "Remember, there's balloons *and* balloons, and one for everybody! Take your choice and take your time. There's many a child got the wrong balloon and his life was never the same after."

"I'll have this one!" said Michael, choosing a yellow one with red markings.

"Well, let me blow it up and you can see if it's the right one!" said the Balloon Woman.

She took it from him and with one gigantic puff blew it up. Zip! There it was! You would hardly think such a tiny person could have so much breath in her body. The yellow balloon, neatly marked with red, bobbed at the end of its string.

"But, I say!" said Michael staring. "It's got my name on it!"

And, sure enough, the red markings on the balloon were letters spelling out the two words—"MICHAEL BANKS."

"Aha!" cackled the Balloon Woman. "What did I tell you? You took your time and the choice was right!"

"See if mine is!" said Jane, handing the Balloon Woman a limp blue balloon.

She puffed and blew it up and there appeared across the fat blue globe the words "JANE CAROLINE BANKS" in large white letters.

"Is that your name, my deary-duck?" said the Balloon Woman.

Jane nodded.

The Balloon Woman laughed to herself, a thin, old cackling laugh, as Jane took the balloon from her and bounced it on the air.

"Me! Me!" cried John and Barbara, plunging fat hands among the balloon-cases. John drew out a pink one and, as she blew it up, the Balloon Woman smiled. There, round the balloon, the words could clearly be seen. "JOHN AND BARBARA BANKS— ONE BETWEEN THEM BECAUSE THEY ARE TWINS."

"But," said Jane, "I don't understand. How did you know? You never saw us before."

"Ah, my deary-duck, didn't I tell you there were balloons *and* balloons and that these were extra-special?"

"But did you put the names on them?" said Michael.

"I?" the old woman chuckled. "Nary I!"

"Then who did?"

"Ask me another, my deary-duck! All I know is that the names *are* there! And there's a balloon for everybody in the world if only they choose properly."

"One for Mary Poppins, too?"

The Balloon Woman, cocked her head and looked at Mary Poppins with a curious smile.

"Let her try!" She rocked herself on her little stool. "Take your choice and take your time! Choose and see!"

Mary Poppins sniffed importantly. Her hand hovered for a moment over the empty balloons and then pounced on a red one. She held it out at arm's length and, to their astonishment, the children saw it slowly filling with air of its' own accord. Larger and larger it grew till it became the size of Michael's. But still it swelled until it was three times as large as any other balloon. And across it appeared in letters of gold the two words "MARY POPPINS."

The red balloon bounced through the air and the old woman tied a string to it and with a little cackling laugh, handed it back to Mary Poppins.

Up into the dancing air danced the four balloons. They tugged at their strings as though they wanted to be free of their moorings. The wind caught them and flung them backwards and forwards, to the North, to the South, to the East, to the West.

"Balloons *and* balloons, my deary-ducks! One for everybody if only they knew it!" cried the Balloon Woman, happily.

At that moment an elderly gentleman in a top hat, turning in at the Park Gates, looked across and saw the balloons. The children saw him give a little start. Then he hurried up to the Balloon Woman.

"How much?" he said, jingling his money in his pocket.

"Sevenpence halfpenny. Take your choice and take your time!"

He took a brown one and the Balloon Woman blew it up. The words "The Honourable WILLIAM WETHERILL WILKINS" appeared on it in green letters.

"Good Gracious!" said the elderly gentleman. "Good gracious, that's *my* name!"

"You choose well, my deary-duck. Balloons *and* balloons!" said the old woman.

The elderly gentleman stared at his balloon as it tugged at it's string.

"Extraordinary!" he said, and blew his nose with a trumpeting sound. "Forty years ago, when I was a boy, I tried to buy a balloon here. But they wouldn't let me. Said they couldn't afford it. Forty years—and it's been waiting for me all this time. Most extraordinary!"

And he hurried away, bumping into the arch because his eyes were fixed on the balloon. The children saw him giving little excited leaps in the air as he went.

"Look at him!" cried Michael as the Elderly Gentleman bobbed higher and higher. But at that moment his own balloon began pulling at the string and he felt himself lifted off his feet.

"Hello, hello! How funny! Mine's doing it, too!"

"Balloons *and* balloons, my deary-duck!" said the Balloon Woman and broke into her cackling laugh as the Twins, both holding their balloon by its single string, bounced off the ground.

"I'm going, I'm going!" shrieked Jane as she, too, was borne upwards.

"Home, please!" said Mary Poppins.

Immediately, the red balloon soared up, dragging Mary Poppins after it. Up and down she bounced, with Annabel and the parcels in her arms. Through the Gates and above the path the red balloon bore

Mary Poppins, her hat very straight, her hair very tidy and her feet as trimly walking the air as they usually walked the earth. Jane and Michael and the

Twins, tugged jerkily up and down by their balloons, followed her.

"Oh, oh, oh!" cried Jane as she was whirled past

the branch of an elm tree, "What a *delicious* feeling!"

"I feel as if I were made of air!" said Michael, knocking into a Park seat and bouncing off it again. "What a lovely way to go home!"

"O-o-h! E-e-eh!" squeaked the Twins, tossing and bobbing together.

"Best foot forward, please, and don't dawdle!" said Mary Poppins, looking fiercely over her shoulder, for all the world as if they were walking sedately on the ground instead of being tugged through the air.

Past the Park Keeper's house they went and down the Lime Walk. The Elderly Gentleman was there bouncing along ahead of them.

Michael turned for a moment and looked behind him.

"Look, Jane, look! Everybody's got one!"

She turned. In the distance a group of people, all carrying balloons, were being jerked up and down in the air.

"The Ice Cream Man has bought one!" she cried, staring and just missing a statue.

"Yes, and the Sweep! And there—do you see?—is Miss Lark!"

Across the lawn a familiar figure came bouncing, hatted and gloved, and holding a balloon bearing the name "LUCINDA EMILY LARK." She bobbed across the Elm Walk, looking very pleased and dignified, and disappeared round the edge of a fountain.

By this time the Park was filling with people and every one of them had a balloon with a name on it and every one was bouncing in the air.

"Heave ho, there! Room for the Admiral! Where's

my port? Heave ho!" shouted a huge, nautical voice as Admiral and Mrs. Boom went rolling through the air. They held the string of a large white balloon with their name on it in blue letters.

"Masts and mizzens! Cockles and shrimps! Haul away, my hearties!" roared Admiral Boom, carefully avoiding a large oak tree.

The crowd of balloons and people grew thicker. There was hardly a patch of air in the Park that was not rainbowy with balloons. Jane and Michael could see Mary Poppins threading her way primly among them and they, too, hurried through the throng, with John and Barbara bobbing at their heels.

"Oh, dear! Oh, dear! My balloon won't bounce me. I must have chosen the wrong one!" said a voice at Jane's elbow.

An old-fashioned lady with a quill in her hat and a feather boa round her neck was standing on the path just below Jane. At her feet lay a purple balloon across which was written in letters of gold, "THE PRIME MINISTER."

"What shall I do?" she cried. "The old woman at the Gates said 'Take your choice and take your time, my deary-duck!' And I did. But I've got the wrong one. *I'm* not the Prime Minister!"

"Excuse me, but I am!" said a voice at her side, as a tall man, very elegantly dressed and carrying a rolled umbrella, stepped up to her.

The lady turned. "Oh, then this is your balloon! Let me see if you've got mine!"

The Prime Minister, whose balloon was not bounc-

ing him at all, showed it to her. Its name was "LADY
MURIEL BRIGHTON-JONES."

"Yes, you have! We've got mixed!" she cried, and
handing the Prime Minister his balloon, she seized
her own. Presently they were off the ground, and flying among the trees, talking as they went.

"Are you married?" Jane and Michael heard Lady
Muriel ask.

And the Prime Minister answered, "No. I can't
find the right sort of middle-aged lady—not too young
and not too old and rather jolly because I'm so serious
myself."

"Would I do?" said Lady Muriel Brighton-Jones.
"I enjoy myself quite a lot."

"Yes, I think you'd do very nicely," said the Prime
Minister and, hand in hand, they joined the tossing
throng.

By this time the Park was really rather crowded.
Jane and Michael, bobbing across the lawns after
Mary Poppins, constantly bumped into other bouncing figures who had bought balloons from the Balloon
Woman. A tall man, wearing a long moustache, a
blue suit and a helmet, was being tugged through the
air by a balloon marked "POLICE INSPECTOR";
and another, bearing the words "LORD MAYOR"
dragged along a round, fat person in a three-cornered
hat, a red overall and a large brass necklace.

"Move on, please! Don't crowd the Park. Observe
the Regulations! All litter to be Deposited in the
Rubbish Baskets!"

The Park Keeper, roaring and ranting, and holding a small cherry-coloured balloon marked "F.

SMITH," threaded his way through the crowd. With a wave of his hand he moved on two dogs—a bull-dog with the word "CU" written on his balloon and a fox-terrier whose name appeared to be "ALBER-TINE."

"Leave my dogs alone! Or I shall take your number and report you!" cried a lady whose balloon said she was "THE DUCHESS OF MAYFIELD."

But the Park Keeper took no notice and went bobbing by, crying "All Dogs on a Lead! Don't crowd the Park! No Smoking! Observe the Regulations!" 'till his voice was hoarse.

"Where's Mary Poppins?" said Michael, whisking up to Jane.

"There! Just ahead of us!" she replied and pointed to the prim, tidy figure that bounced at the end of the largest balloon in the Park. They followed it homewards.

"Balloons *and* Balloons, my deary-ducks!" cried a cackling voice behind them.

And, turning, they saw the Balloon Woman. Her

By this time the Park was really rather crowded

tray was empty and there was not a balloon anywhere near her, but in spite of that she was flying through the air as though a hundred invisible balloons were drawing her onwards.

"Every one sold!" she screamed as she sped by. "There's a balloon for every one if only they knew it. They took their choice and they took their time! And I've sold the lot! Balloons *and* Balloons."

Her pockets jingled richly as she flew by and, standing still in the air, Jane and Michael watched the small, withered figure shooting past the bobbing balloons, past the Prime Minister and the Lord Mayor, past Mary Poppins and Annabel, until the tiny shape grew tinier still and the Balloon Woman disappeared into the distance.

"Balloons and balloons, my deary-ducks!" The faint echo came drifting back to them.

"Step along, please!" said Mary Poppins. They flocked round her, all four of them. Annabel, rocked by the movement of Mary Poppins' balloon, nestled closer to her and went to sleep.

The gate of Number Seventeen stood open, the front door was ajar. Mary Poppins, leaping neatly and bouncing primly, passed through and up the stairs. The children followed, jumping and bobbing. And when they reached the nursery door, their four pairs of feet clattered noisily to the ground. Mary Poppins floated down and landed without a sound.

"Oh, what a *lovely* afternoon!" said Jane, rushing to fling her arms round Mary Poppins.

"Well, that's more than *you* are, at this moment.

Brush your hair, please. I don't care for scarecrows,"
Mary Poppins said tartly.

"I feel like a balloon myself," said Michael joyfully, "All airy-fairy-free!"

"I'd be sorry for the fairy that looked like you!"
said Mary Poppins. "Go and wash your hands. You're
no better than a sweep!"

When they came back, clean and tidy, the four
balloons were resting against the ceiling, their strings
firmly moored behind the picture over the mantel-
piece.

Michael gazed up at them—his own yellow one,
Jane's blue, the Twins' pink and Mary Poppins' red.
They were very still. No breath of wind moved them.

Light and bright, steady and still, they leaned against the ceiling.

"I wonder!" said Michael softly, half to himself.

"You wonder what?" said Mary Poppins, sorting out her parcels.

"I wonder if it would all have happened if you hadn't been with us."

Mary Poppins sniffed.

"I shouldn't wonder if you didn't wonder much too much!" she replied.

And with that Michael had to be content.

9

NELLIE-RUBINA

"I DON'T believe it will ever stop—ever!"
Jane put down her copy of *Robinson Crusoe* and gazed gloomily out of the window.

The snow fell steadily, drifting down in large soft flakes, covering the Park and the pavements and the houses in Cherry Tree Lane with its thick white mantle. It had not stopped snowing for a week and in all that time the children had not once been able to go out.

"I don't mind—not very much." said Michael from the floor where he was busy arranging the animals of his Noah's Ark. "We can be Esquimos and eat whales."

"Silly—how could we get whales when it's too snowy even to go and buy cough drops!"

"They might come nere. Whales do, sometimes," he retorted.

"How do you know?"

"Well, I don't *know*, exactly. But they might. Jane, where's the second giraffe. Oh, here he is—under the tiger!"

He put the two giraffes into the Ark together.

"The Animals went in Two-by-Two,
   The Elephant and the Kangaroo,"

sang Michael. And, because he hadn't got a kangaroo, he sent an antelope in with the elephant and
Mr. and Mrs. Noah behind them to keep order.

"I wonder why they never have any relatives!" he
remarked presently.

"*Who* don't?" said Jane crossly, for she didn't want
to be disturbed.

"The Noahs. I've never seen them with a daughter
or a son or an uncle or an aunt. Why?"

"Because they don't have them," said Jane. "Do
be quiet."

"Well, I was only remarking. Can't I remark if I
want to?"

He was beginning to feel cross now, and very tired
of being cooped up in the Nursery. He scrambled to
his feet and swaggered over to Jane.

"I only said——" he began annoyingly, jogging the
hand that held the book.

But at that, Jane's patience gave way and she
hurled *Robinson Crusoe* across the room.

"How dare you disturb me?" she shouted, turning
on Michael.

"How dare you not let me make a remark?"

"I didn't!"

"You did!"

And in another moment Jane was shaking Michael
furiously by the shoulders and he had gripped a
great handful of her hair.

"WHAT IS ALL THIS?"

Mary Poppins stood in the doorway, glowering down at them.

They fell apart.

"She sh-sh-shook me!" wailed Michael, but he looked guiltily at Mary Poppins.

"He p-p-pulled my hair" sobbed Jane, hiding her head in her arms, for she dared not face that stern gaze.

Mary Poppins stalked into the room. She had a pile of coats, caps and mufflers on her arm and the Twins, round-eyed and interested, were at her heels.

"I would rather," she remarked with a sniff, "have a family of Cannibals to look after. They'd be more human!"

"But she did sh-sh-shake me——" Michael began again.

"Tell-Tale-Tit, Your tongue shall be slit!" jeered Mary Poppins. Then, as he seemed to be going to protest, "Don't dare answer back!" she said warningly and tossed him his overcoat. "Get your things on, please! We're going out!"

"Out?"

They could hardly believe their ears! But at the sound of that word all their crossness melted away. Michael, buttoning up his leggings, felt sorry he had annoyed Jane and looked across to find her putting on her woolen cap and smiling at him.

"Hooray, hooray, hooray!" They shouted, stamping and clapping their woolen-gloved hands.

"Cannibals!" she said fiercely and pushed them in front of her down the stairs. . . .

The snow was no longer falling but was piled in heavy drifts all over the garden and beyond, in the Park, it lay over everything like a thick white quilt. The naked branches of the Cherry trees were covered with a glistening rind of snow and the Park railings, that had once been green and slender, were now white and rather woolly.

Down the garden path Robertson Ay was languidly trailing his shovel, pausing every few inches to take a long rest. He was wearing an old overcoat of Mr. Banks' that was much too big for him. As soon as he had shovelled the snow from one piece of path, the coat, drifting behind him, swept a new drift of snow over the cleared patch.

But the children raced past him and down to the gate, crying and shouting and waving their arms.

Outside in the Lane everybody who lived in it seemed to be taking the air.

"Ahoy there, shipmates!" cried a roaring, soaring voice as Admiral Boom came up and shook them all by the hand. He was wrapped from head to foot in a large Inverness cape and his nose was redder than they had ever seen it.

"Good day!" said Jane and Michael politely.

"Port and starboard!" cried the Admiral. "I don't call *this* a good day. Hur-rrrrrumph! A hideous, hoary, land lubberly sort of a day, I call it. Why doesn't the Spring come? Tell me that!"

"Now, Andrew! Now, Willoughby! Keep close to Mother!"

Miss Lark, muffled up in a long fur coat and wearing a fur hat like a tea-cosy, was taking a walk with her two dogs.

"Good morning, everybody!" She greeted them fussily. "*What* weather! *Where* has the sun gone? And *why* doesn't the Spring come?"

"Don't ask me, Ma'am!" shouted Admiral Boom. "No affair of mine. You should go to sea. Always good weather there! Go to sea!"

"Oh, Admiral Boom, I couldn't do that! I haven't the time. I am just off to buy Andrew and Willoughby a fur coat each."

A look of shame and horror passed between the two dogs.

"Fur coats!" roared the Admiral. "Blast my binnacle! Fur coats for a couple of mongrels? Heave her over! Port, I say! Up with the Anchor! Fur coats!"

"Admiral! Admiral!" cried Miss Lark, stopping her ears with her hands. "Such *language!* Please, please remember I am not used to it. And my dogs are *not* mongrels. Not at all! One has a long pedigree and the other has at least a Kind Heart. Mongrels, indeed!"

And she hurried away, talking to herself in a high, angry voice, with Andrew and Willoughby sidling behind her, swinging their tails and looking very uncomfortable and ashamed.

The Ice Cream Man trundled past on his cycle, going at a terrific rate and ringing his bell madly.

"DON'T STOP ME OR I SHALL CATCH COLD" said the notice in front of his cart.

"Whenever's that there Spring coming?" shouted the Ice Cream Man to the Sweep who at that moment came trudging round the corner. To keep out the cold he had completely covered himself with brushes so that he looked more like a porcupine than a man.

"Bur-rum, bur-rum, bumble!" came the voice of the Sweep through the brushes.

"What's that?" said the Ice Cream Man.

"Bumble!"

The Sweep remarked, disappearing in at Miss Lark's Tradesman's Entrance.

In the gateway to the Park stood the Keeper, waving his arms and stamping his feet and blowing on his hands.

"Need a bit of Spring, don't we?" he said cheerfully to Mary Poppins as she and the children passed through.

"*I'm* quite satisfied!" replied Mary Poppins primly, tossing her head.

"*Self*-satisfied, I'd call it," muttered the Keeper. But as he said it behind his hand, only Jane and Michael heard him.

Michael dawdled behind. He stooped and gathered up a handful of snow and rolled it between his palms.

"Jane, dear!" he called in a wheedling voice. "I've got something for you!"

She turned, and the snowball, whizzing through the air, caught her on the shoulder. With a squeal she began to burrow in the snow and presently there were snowballs flying through the air in every direction. And in and out, among the tossing, glistening balls, walked Mary Poppins, very prim and neat, and thinking to herself how handsome she looked in her large woolen gloves and her rabbit-skin coat.

And just as she was thinking that, a large snowball grazed past the brim of her hat and landed right on her nose.

"Oh!" screamed Michael, putting up both hands to his mouth. "I didn't mean to, Mary Poppins! I didn't, really. It was for Jane."

Mary Poppins turned and her face, as it appeared through the fringe of broken snowball, was terrible.

"Mary Poppins," he said earnestly. "I'm sorry. It was a Naccident!"

"A Naccident or not!" she retorted. "That's the end of *your* snowballing. Naccident, indeed! A *Zulu* would have better manners!"

She plucked the remains of the snowball from her neck and rolled them into a small ball between her woolen palms. Then she flung the ball right across the snowy lawn and went stamping haughtily after it.

"Now you've done it," whispered Jane.

"I didn't mean to," Michael whispered back.

"I know. But you know what she is!"

Mary Poppins, arriving at the place where the snowball had fallen, picked it up and threw it again, a long powerful throw.

"Where is she going?" said Michael suddenly. For the snowball was bowling away under the trees and, instead of keeping to the path, Mary Poppins was hurrying after it. Every now and then she dodged a little fall of snow as it tumbled softly from a branch.

"I can hardly keep up!" said Michael, stumbling over his own feet.

Mary Poppins quickened her steps. The children panted behind her. And when at last they caught up with the snowball they found it lying beside the strangest building they had ever seen.

"I don't remember seeing this house before!" exclaimed Jane, her eyes wide with surprise.

"It's more like an Ark than a house," said Michael, staring.

The house stood solidly in the snow, moored by a thick rope to the trunk of a tree. Round it, like a verandah, ran a long narrow deck and its high peaked roof was painted bright scarlet. But the most curious thing about it was that though it had several windows there was not a single door.

"Where *are* we?" said Jane, full of curiosity and excitement.

Mary Poppins made no reply. She led the way along the deck and stopped in front of a notice that said,

"KNOCK THREE AND A HALF TIMES"

"What is half a knock?" whispered Michael to Jane.

"Sh!" she said, nodding towards Mary Poppins. And her nod said as clearly as if she had spoken—"We're on the brink of an Adventure. Don't spoil it by asking questions!"

Mary Poppins, seizing the knocker that hung above the notice, swung it upwards and knocked three times against the wall. Then, taking it daintily between the finger and thumb of her woolen glove, she gave the merest, tiniest, smallest, gentlest tap.

Like this.

RAP! RAP! RAP! .   .   .   Tap.

Immediately, as though it had been listening and waiting for that signal, the roof of the building flew back on its hinges.

"Goodness Graciousness!" Michael could not restrain the exclamation for the wind of the roof, as it swung open, nearly lifted his hat off.

Mary Poppins walked to the end of the narrow deck and began to climb a small, steep ladder. At the top she turned, and looking very solemn and important, beckoned with a woolly finger.

"Step up, please!"

The four children hurried after her.

"Jump!" cried Mary Poppins, leaping down from the top of the ladder into the house. She turned and caught the Twins as they came tumbling over the edge with Jane and Michael after them. And as soon as they were all safely inside, the roof closed over again and shut with a little click.

They gazed round them. Four pairs of eyes popped with surprise.

"*What* a funny room!" exclaimed Jane.

But it was really more than funny. It was extraordinary. The only piece of furniture in it was a large counter that ran along one end of the room. The walls were white-washed and, leaning against them, were piles of wood cut into the shape of trees and branches and all painted green. Small wooden sprays of leaves, newly painted and polished, were scattered about the floor. And several notices hung from the walls saying:

"MIND THE PAINT!"
or
"DON'T TOUCH!"
or
"KEEP OFF THE GRASS!"

But this was not all.

In one corner stood a flock of wooden sheep with the dye still wet on their fleeces. Crowded in another were small stiff groups of flowers—yellow aconites, green-and-white snowdrops and bright blue scyllas. All of them looked very shiny and sticky as though they had been newly varnished. So did the wooden birds and butterflies that were neatly piled in a third corner. So did the flat white wooden clouds that leant against the counter.

But the enormous jar that stood on a shelf at the end of the room was not painted. It was made of green glass and filled to the brim with hundreds of small flat shapes of every kind and colour.

"You're quite right, Jane," said Michael staring. "It *is* a funny room!"

"Funny!" said Mary Poppins, looking as though he had said something insulting.

"Well—peculiar."

"PECULIAR?"

Michael hesitated. He could not find the right word.

"What I meant was——"

"I think it's a lovely room, Mary Poppins——" said Jane, hastily coming to the rescue.

"Yes it is," said Michael, very relieved. "And—" he added cleverly, "*I* think you look very nice in that hat."

He watched her carefully. Yes, her face was a little softer—there were even faint beginnings of a conceited smile around her mouth.

"Humph!" she remarked and turned towards the end of the room.

"Nellie-Rubina!" she called. "Where are you? We've arrived!"

"Coming! Coming!"

The highest, thinnest voice they had ever heard seemed to rise up from beneath the counter. And, presently, from the same direction as the voice, a head, topped with a small flat hat, popped up. It was followed by a round, rather solid body that held in one hand a pot of red paint and in the other a plain wooden tulip.

Surely, surely, thought Jane and Michael, this was the strangest person they had ever seen.

From her face and size she seemed to be quite young but somehow she looked as though she were made, not of flesh, but of wood. Her stiff, shiny black hair seemed to have been carved on her head and then painted. Her eyes were like small black holes drilled in her face and, surely that bright pink patch on her shiny cheek was paint!

"Well, Miss Poppins!" said this curious person, her red lips glistening as she smiled. "This *is* nice of you, I must say!" And putting down the paint and the tulip, she came round the counter and shook hands with Mary Poppins.

Then it was that the children noticed she had no legs at all! She was quite solid from the waist downwards and moved with a rolling motion by means of a round flat disc that was where her feet should have been.

"Not at all, Nellie-Rubina," said Mary Poppins, with unusual politeness. "It is a Pleasure and a Treat!"

"We've been expecting you, of course," Nellie-Rubina went on, "because we wanted you to help with the——" She broke off, for not only had Mary Poppins flashed her a warning look, but she had caught sight of the children.

"Oh," she cried in her high friendly voice. "You've brought Jane and Michael! And the Twins, too. What a surprise!" She bowled across and shook hands jerkily with them all.

"Do you know us, then?" said Michael, staring at her amazed.

"Oh, dear me, yes!" she trilled gaily. "I've often heard my Father and Mother speak of you. Pleased to make your acquaintance." She laughed, and insisted on shaking hands all round again.

"I thought, Nellie-Rubina," said Mary Poppins, "that maybe you could spare an ounce of Conversations."

"Most certainly!" said Nellie-Rubina, smiling and

rolling towards the counter. "To do anything for *you*, Miss Poppins, is an Honour and a Joy!"

"But can you have conversation by the ounce?" said Jane.

"Yes, indeed. By the pound, too. Or the ton, if you like." Nellie-Rubina broke off. She lifted her arms to the large jar on the shelf. They were just too short to reach it. "Tch, tch, tch! Not long enough. I must have a bit added. In the meantime, I'll get my Uncle to lift them down. Uncle Dodger! Uncle Dod-GER!"

She screamed the last words through a door behind the counter and immediately an odd-looking person appeared.

He was as round as Nellie-Rubina, but much older and with a sadder sort of face. He, too, had a little flat hat on his head and his coat was tightly buttoned across a chest as woodeny as Nellie-Rubina's. And Jane and Michael could see, as his apron swung aside for a moment, that, like his niece, he was solid from the waist downwards. In his hand he carried a wooden cuckoo half-covered with grey paint and there were splashes of the same paint on his own nose.

"You called, my dear?" he asked, in a mild, respectful voice.

Then, he saw Mary Poppins.

"Ah, here you are at last, Miss Poppins! Nellie-Rubina *will* be pleased. She's been expecting you to help us with——"

He caught sight of the children and broke off suddenly.

"Oh, I beg pardon. I didn't know there was Company, my dear! I'll just go and finish this bird——"

"You will not, Uncle Dodger!" said Nellie-Rubina,

sharply. "I want the Conversations lifted down. Will you be so good?"

Although she had such a jolly, cheerful face, the children noticed that when she spoke to her Uncle she gave orders rather than asked favours.

Uncle Dodger sprang forward as swiftly as anybody could who had no legs.

"Certainly, my dear, certainly!" He lifted his arms jerkily and set the jar on the counter.

"In front of me, please!" ordered Nellie-Rubina haughtily.

Fussily Uncle Dodger edged the Jar along.

"There you are, my dear, begging your pardon!"

"Are *those* the Conversations?" asked Jane, pointing to the Jar. "They look more like sweets."

"So they are, Miss! They're Conversation Sweets," said Uncle Dodger, dusting the jar with his apron.

"Does one eat them?" inquired Michael.

Uncle Dodger, glancing cautiously at Nellie-Rubina, leaned across the counter.

"*One* does," he whispered behind his hand. "But *I* don't, being only an Uncle-by-Marriage. But she——" he nodded respectfully towards his niece, "she's the Eldest Daughter and a Direct Descendant!"

Neither Jane nor Michael knew in the least what he meant but they nodded politely.

"Now," cried Nellie-Rubina gaily as she unscrewed the lid of the Jar. "Who'll choose first?"

Jane thrust in her hand and brought out a flat star-shaped sweet rather like a peppermint.

"There's writing on it!" she exclaimed.

Nellie-Rubina shrieked with laughter. "Of course there is! It's a Conversation! Read it."

"You're My Fancy," read Jane aloud.

"How *very* nice!" tinkled Nellie-Rubina, pushing the jar towards Michael. He drew out a pink sweet shaped like a shell.

"I Love You. Do You Love Me?" He spelled out.

"Ha, ha! That's a good one! Yes, I do!" Nellie-Rubina laughed loudly, and gave him a quick kiss that left a sticky patch of paint on his cheek.

John's yellow Conversation read "Deedle, deedle, dumpling!" and on Barbara's was written in large letters, "Shining-bright and airy."

"And so you are!" cried Nellie-Rubina, smiling at her over the counter.

"Now you, Miss Poppins!" And as Nellie-Rubina tipped the Jar towards Mary Poppins, Jane and Michael noticed a curious, understanding look pass between them.

Off came the large woolen glove and Mary Poppins, shutting her eyes, put in her hand and scrabbled for a moment among the Conversations. Then her fingers closed on a white one shaped like a half-moon and she held it out in front of her.

"Ten o'clock to-night," said Jane, reading the inscription aloud.

Uncle Dodger rubbed his hands together.

"That's right. That's the time when we——"

"Uncle Dod-GER!" cried Nellie-Rubina in a warning voice.

The smile died away from his face and left it sadder than before.

"Begging your pardon, my dear!" He said humbly. "I'm an old man, I'm afraid, and I sometimes say the wrong thing—beg pardon." He looked very ashamed of himself but Jane and Michael could not see that he had done anything very wrong.

"Well," said Mary Poppins, slipping her Conversation carefully into her hand-bag. "If you'll excuse us, Nellie-Rubina, I think we'd better be going!"

"Oh, must you?" Nellie-Rubina rolled a little on her disc. "It has been Such a Satisfaction! Still," she glanced out of a window, "it might snow again and keep you imprisoned here. And you wouldn't like that, would you?" she trilled, turning to the children.

"I would," said Michael, stoutly. "I would love it. And then, perhaps, I'd find out what these are for." He pointed to the painted branches, the sheep and birds and flowers.

"Those? Oh, those are just decorations," said Nellie-Rubina, airily dismissing them with a jerky wave of her hand.

"But what do you do with them?"

Uncle Dodger leaned eagerly across the counter.

"Well, you see, we take them out and——"

"Uncle Dod-GER!" Nellie-Rubina's dark eyes were snapping dangerously.

"Oh—dear! There I go again. Always speaking out of my turn. I'm too old, that's what it is," said Uncle Dodger mournfully.

Nellie-Rubina gave him an angry look. Then she turned smiling to the children.

"Good-bye," she said, jerkily shaking hands. "I'll remember our Conversations. You're my Fancy, I love You, Deedle-deedle and Shining-bright!"

"You've forgotten Mary Poppins' Conversation. It's 'Ten o'clock to-night,'" Michael reminded her.

"Ah, but *she* won't!" said Uncle Dodger, smiling happily.

"Uncle Dod-GER!"

"Oh, begging your pardon, begging your pardon!"

"Good-bye!" said Mary Poppins. She patted her hand-bag importantly and another strange look passed between her and Nellie-Rubina.

"Good-bye, good-bye!"

When Jane and Michael thought about it afterwards, they could not remember how they had got out of that curious room. One moment they were inside it saying good-bye to Nellie-Rubina and the next they were out in the snow again, licking their Conversations and hurrying after Mary Poppins.

"Do you know, Michael," said Jane, "I believe that sweet was a message."

"Which one? Mine?"

"No. The one Mary Poppins chose."

"You mean——?"

"I think something is going to happen at ten o'clock to-night and I'm going to stay awake and see."

"Then so will I," said Michael.

"Come along, please! Keep up!" said Mary Poppins. "I haven't *all* day to waste. . . ."

Jane was dreaming deeply. And in her dream somebody was calling her name in a small urgent voice. She sat up with a start to find Michael standing beside her in his pyjamas.

"You said you'd stay awake!" he whispered accusingly.

"What? Where? Why? Oh, it's you, Michael! Well, you said you would, too."

"Listen!" he said.

There was a sound of somebody tip-toeing in the next room.

Jane drew in her breath sharply. "Quick! Get back into bed. Pretend to be asleep. Hurry!"

With a bound Michael was under the blankets. In the darkness he and Jane held their breath, listening.

From the other Nursery, the door opened stealthily. The thin gap of light widened and grew larger. A head came round the edge and peered into the room. Then somebody slipped through and silently shut the door behind her.

Mary Poppins, wrapped in her fur coat and holding her shoes in her hands, tip-toed through their room.

They lay still, listening to her steps hurrying down the stairs. Far away the key of the front door scraped in its lock. There was a scurry of steps on the garden path and the front gate clicked.

And at that moment the clock struck ten!

Out of bed they sprang and rushed into the other Nursery where the windows opened on the Park.

The night was black and splendid, lit with high swinging stars. But to-night it was not stars they were looking for. If Mary Poppins' Conversation had really been a message, there was something more interesting to be seen.

"Look!" Jane gave a little gulp of excitement and pointed.

Over in the Park, just by the entrance gate, stood the curious ark-shaped building, loosely moored to a tree-trunk.

"But how did it get *there?*" said Michael staring.

"It was at the other side of the Park this morning."

Jane did not reply. She was too busy watching.

The roof of the Ark was open and on the top of the ladder stood Nellie-Rubina, balancing on her round disc. From inside Uncle Dodger was handing up to her bundle after bundle of painted wooden branches.

"Ready, Miss Poppins?" tinkled Nellie-Rubina, passing an armful down to Mary Poppins who was standing on the deck waiting to receive them.

The air was so clear and still that Jane and Michael, crouched in the window-seat, could hear every word.

Suddenly there was a loud noise inside the Ark as a wooden shape clattered to the floor.

"Uncle Dod-GER! Be careful, please! They're fragile!" said Nellie-Rubina sternly. And Uncle Dodger, as he lifted out a pile of painted clouds, replied apologetically,

"Begging your pardon, my dear!"

The flock of wooden sheep came next, all very stiff and solid. And last of all, the birds, butterflies and flowers.

"That's the lot!" said Uncle Dodger, heaving himself up through the open roof. Under his arm he carried the wooden cuckoo, now entirely covered with grey paint. And in his hand swung a large green paint-pot.

"Very well," said Nellie-Rubina. "Now, if you're ready, Miss Poppins, we'll begin!"

And then began one of the strangest pieces of work Jane and Michael had ever seen. Never, never, they thought, would they forget it, even if they lived to be ninety.

From the pile of painted wood Nellie-Rubina and Mary Poppins each took a long spray of leaves and, leaping into the air, attached them swiftly to the naked frosty branches of the trees. The sprays seemed to clip on easily for it did not take more than a min-

ute to attach them. And as each was slipped into place, Uncle Dodger would spring up and neatly dab a spot of green paint at the point where the spray joined the tree.

"My Goodness *Goodness*!" exclaimed Jane, as Nellie-Rubina sailed lightly up to the top of a tall poplar and fixed a large branch there. But Michael was too astonished to say anything.

All over the Park went the three, jumping up to the tallest branch as if they were on springs. And in no time every tree in the Park was decked out with wooden sprays of leaves and neatly finished off with dabs of paint from Uncle Dodger's brush.

Every now and then Jane and Michael heard Nellie-Rubina's shrill voice crying.

"Uncle Dod-GER! Be CAREFUL!" and Uncle Dodger's voice begging her pardon.

And now Nellie-Rubina and Mary Poppins took up in their arms the flat white wooden clouds. With these they soared higher than ever before, shooting right above the trees and pressing the clouds carefully against the sky.

"They're sticking, they're sticking!" cried Michael excitedly, dancing on the window seat. And, sure enough, against the sparkling, darkling sky the flat white clouds stuck fast.

"Who-o-o-op!" cried Nellie-Rubina as she swooped down. "Now for the sheep!"

Very carefully, on a snowy strip of lawn, they set up the wooden flock, huddling the larger sheep together with the stiff white lambs among them.

"We're getting on!" Jane and Michael heard Mary Poppins say, as she put the last lamb on its legs.

"I don't know what we'd have done without you, Miss Poppins, indeed I don't!" said Nellie-Rubina, pleasantly. Then, in quite a different voice,

"Flowers, please, Uncle Dodger! And look sharp!"

"Here, my dear!" He rolled hurriedly up to her, his apron bulging with snow-drops, scyllas and aconites.

"Oh, look! Look!" Jane cried, hugging herself delightedly. For Nellie-Rubina was sticking the wooden

Against the sparkling, darkling sky the flat white clouds stuck fast

shapes round the edge of an empty flower-bed. Round and round she rolled, planting her wooden border and reaching up her hand again and again for a fresh flower from Uncle Dodger's apron.

"That's neat!" said Mary Poppins admiringly, and Jane and Michael were astonished at the pleasant friendly tone of her voice.

"Yes, isn't it?" trilled Nellie-Rubina, brushing the snow from her hands, "Quite a Sight! What's left, Uncle Dodger?"

"The birds, my dear, and the butterflies!" He held out his apron. Nellie-Rubina and Mary Poppins seized the remaining wooden shapes and ran swiftly about the Park, setting the birds on branches or in nests and tossing the butterflies into the air. And the curious thing was that they *stayed* there, poised above the earth, their bright patches of paint showing clearly in the starlight.

"There! I think that's all!" said Nellie-Rubina, standing still on her disc, with her hands on her hips, as she gazed round at her handiwork.

"One thing more, my dear!" said Uncle Dodger.

And, rather unevenly, as though the evening's work had made him feel old and tired, he bowled towards the ash tree near the Park Gates. He took the cuckoo from under his arm and set it on a branch among the wooden leaves.

"There, my bonny! There, my dove!" he said, nodding his head at the bird.

"Uncle Dod-GER! When *will* you learn? It's *not* a dove. It's a cuckoo!"

He bent his head humbly.

"A dove of a cuckoo—that's what I meant. Begging your pardon, my dear!"

"Well, now, Miss Poppins, I'm afraid we must really be going!" said Nellie-Rubina and, rolling towards Mary Poppins, she took the pink face between her two woodeny hands and kissed it.

"See you soon, Tra-la!" she cried airily, bowling along the deck of the Ark and up the little ladder. At the top she turned and waved her hand jerkily to Mary Poppins. Then, with a woodeny clatter, she leapt down and disappeared inside.

"Uncle Dod-GER! Come along! Don't keep me waiting!" her thin voice floated back.

"Coming, my dear, coming! Begging your pardon!" Uncle Dodger rolled toward the deck, shaking hands with Mary Poppins on the way. The wooden cuckoo stared out from its leafy branch. He flung it a sad, affectionate glance. Then his flat disc rose in the air and echoed woodenly as he landed inside. The roof flew down and shut with a click.

"Let her go!" came Nellie-Rubina's shrill command from within. Mary Poppins stepped forward and unwound the mooring-rope from the tree. It was immediately drawn in through one of the windows.

"Make way, there, please! Make way!" shouted Nellie-Rubina. Mary Poppins stepped back hurriedly.

Michael clutched Jane's arm excitedly.

"They're off!" he cried, as the Ark rose from the ground and moved top-heavily above the snow. Up it went, rocking drunkenly between the trees. Then it steadied itself and passed lightly up and over the topmost boughs.

A jerky arm waved downwards from one of the windows but before Jane and Michael could be certain whether it was Nellie-Rubina's or Uncle Dodger's the Ark swept into the star-lit air and a corner of the house hid it from view.

Mary Poppins stood for a moment by the Park Gates waving her woollen gloves.

Then she came hurrying across the Lane and up the garden path. The front door key scraped in the lock. A cautious foot-step creaked on the stairs!

"Back to bed, quick!" said Jane. "She mustn't find us here!"

Down from the window-seat and through the door they fled and with two quick jumps landed in their beds. They had just time to put the bed-clothes over their heads before Mary Poppins opened the door quietly and tip-toed through.

Zup! That was her coat being hung on its hook. Crackle! That was her hat rustling down into its paper-bag. But they heard no more. For by the time she had undressed and climbed into her camp bed, Jane and Michael had huggled down under the blankets and were fast asleep. . . .

"Cuckoo! Cuckoo! Cuckoo!"

Across the Lane the soft bird note came floating.

"Jumping giraffes!" cried Mr. Banks, as he lathered his face, "The Spring is here!"

And he flung down his shaving-brush and rushed out into the garden. He gave one look at it and then, flinging back his head, he made a trumpet with his hands.

"Jane! Michael! John! Barbara!" he called up to the Nursery windows. "Come down! The snow's gone and Spring has come!"

They came tumbling down the stairs and out of the front door to find the whole Lane alive with people.

"Ship ahoy!" roared Admiral Boom waving his muffler. "Rope and Rigging! Cockles and Shrimps! Here's the Spring!"

"Well!" said Miss Lark, hurrying out through her gate. "A fine day at last! I was thinking of getting Andrew and Willoughby two pairs of leather boots each, but now the snow's gone I shan't have to!"

At that Andrew and Willoughby looked very relieved and licked her hand to show they were glad she had not disgraced them.

The Ice Cream Man wheeled slowly up and down, keeping an eye open for customers. And to-day his notice board read—

> "Spring has come,
> Rum-ti-tum,
> Stop and buy one,
> Spring has come!"

And the Sweep, carrying only one brush, walked along the Lane, looking from right to left with a satisfied air, as though he himself had arranged the lovely day.

And in the middle of all the excitement Jane and Michael stood still, staring about them.

Everything shone and glistened in the sunlight. There was not a single flake of snow to be seen.

From every branch of every tree, the tender pale-green buds were bursting. Round the edge of the flower-bed just inside the Park fragile green shoots of aconites, snow-drops and scyllas were breaking into a border of yellow, white and blue. Presently the Park Keeper came along and picked a tiny bunch and put them carefully in his button hole.

From flower to flower brightly-coloured butterflies were darting on downy wings, and in the branches thrushes and tits and swallows and finches were singing and building nests.

A flock of sheep with soft young lambs at their heels went by, baa-ing loudly.

And from the bough of the ash tree by the Park Gates came the clear double-noted call—

"Cuckoo! Cuckoo!"

Michael turned to Jane. His eyes were shining.

"So that's what they were doing—Nellie-Rubina and Uncle Dodger and Mary Poppins!"

Jane nodded, gazing wonderingly about her.

Among the faint green smoke of buds a grey body rocked backwards and forwards on the ash-bough.

"Cuckoo! Cuckoo!"

"But—I thought they were all made of painted wood!" said Michael. "Did they come alive in the night, do you think?"

"Perhaps," said Jane.

"Cuckoo! Cuckoo!"

Jane seized Michael's hand and, as though he

guessed the thought in her mind, he ran with her through the garden, across the Lane and into the Park.

"Hi! Where are you going, you two?" called Mr. Banks.

"Ahoy, there, messmates!" roared Admiral Boom.

"You'll get lost!" warned Miss Lark shrilly.

The Ice Cream Man tingled his bell wildly and the Sweep stood staring after them.

But Jane and Michael took no notice. They ran on, right through the Park under the trees to the place where they had first seen the Ark.

They drew up panting. It was cold and shadowy here under the dark branches and the snow had not yet melted. They peered about, seeking, seeking. But there was only a heavy drift of snowflakes spread under the dark green boughs.

"It's really gone, then!" said Michael, gazing round.

"Do you think we only imagined it, Jane?" he asked doubtfully. She bent down suddenly and picked up something from the snow.

"No," she said slowly, "I'm sure we didn't." She held out her hand. In her palm lay a round pink Conversation Sweet. She read out the words.

"Good-bye till Next Year,
NELLIE-RUBINA NOAH."

Michael drew a deep breath.

"So that's who she was! Uncle Dodger said she was the Eldest Daughter. But I never guessed."

"She brought the Spring!" said Jane dreamily, gazing at the Conversation.

"I'll thank you," said a voice behind them "to come home at once and eat your breakfast," said Mary Poppins.

They turned guiltily.

"We were just—" Michael began to explain.

"Then don't," snapped Mary Poppins. She leant over Jane's shoulder and took the Conversation.

"That, I believe, is mine!" she remarked and, putting it in her apron pocket, she led the way home through the Park.

Michael broke off a spray of green buds as he went. He examined them carefully.

"They seem quite real now," he said.

"Perhaps they always were," said Jane.

And a mocking voice came fluting from the ash tree,

"Cuckoo! Cuckoo! Cuckoo!"

IO

MERRY-GO-ROUND

IT HAD been a quiet morning.

More than one person, passing along Cherry Tree Lane, had looked over the fence of Number Seventeen and said—"How very extraordinary! Not a sound!"

Even the house, which usually took no notice of anything, began to feel alarmed.

"Dear me! Dear me!" it said to itself, listening to the silence. "I hope nothing's wrong!"

Downstairs in the Kitchen, Mrs. Brill, with her spectacles on the tip of her nose, was nodding over the newspaper.

On the first-floor landing, Mrs. Banks and Ellen were tidying the Linen-cupboard and counting the sheets.

Upstairs in the Nursery Mary Poppins was quietly clearing away the luncheon things.

"I feel very good and sweet to-day," Jane was saying drowsily, as she lay stretched on the floor in a patch of sunlight.

"That must be a change!" remarked Mary Poppins with a sniff.

Michael took the last chocolate out of the box Aunt Flossie had given him for his sixth birthday last week.

Should he offer it to Jane? He wondered. Or to the Twins? Or Mary Poppins?

No. After all, it had been *his* birthday.

"Last, lucky last!" he said quickly and popped it into his own mouth. "And I wish there were more!" he added regretfully, gazing into the empty box.

"All good things come to an end, sometime," said Mary Poppins primly.

He cocked his head on one side and looked up at her.

"*You* don't!" he said daringly. "And you're a good thing."

The beginnings of a satisfied smile glimmered at the corners of her mouth but it disappeared as quickly as it had come.

"That's as may be," she retorted. "Nothing lasts for ever."

Jane looked round, startled.

If nothing lasted for ever it meant that Mary Poppins——

"Nothing?" she said uneasily.

"Nothing at all," snapped Mary Poppins.

And as if she had guessed what was in Jane's mind she went to the mantel-piece and took down her large Thermometer. Then she pulled her carpet-bag from under the camp-bed and popped the Thermometer into it.

Jane sat up quickly.

"Mary Poppins, why are you doing that?"

Mary Poppins gave her a curious look.

"Because," she said priggishly. "I was always taught

to be tidy." And she pushed the carpet-bag under the bed again.

Jane sighed. Her heart felt tight and heavy in her chest.

"I feel rather sad and anxious," she whispered to Michael.

"I expect you had too much steam pudding!" he retorted.

"No, it's not that kind of a feeling——" she began and broke off suddenly for a knock had sounded at the door.

Tap! Tap!

"Come in!" called Mary Poppins.

Robertson Ay stood there yawning.

"Do you know what?" he said sleepily.

"No, what?"

"There's a Merry-go-round in the Park!"

"That's no news to me!" snapped Mary Poppins.

"A Fair?" cried Michael excitedly. "With swinging-boats and a Hoop-la?"

"No," said Robertson Ay, solemnly shaking his head. "A Merry-go-round, all by itself. Came last night. Thought you would like to know."

He shuffled languidly to the door and closed it after him.

Jane sprang up, her anxiety forgotten.

"Oh, Mary Poppins, may we go?"

"Say Yes, Mary Poppins, say Yes!" cried Michael dancing round her.

She turned, balancing a tray of plates and cups on her arm.

"*I* am going," she remarked, calmly. "Because I have the fare. I don't know about you."

"There's sixpence in my money-box!" said Jane eagerly.

"Oh, Jane, lend me twopence!" pleaded Michael. He had spent all his money the day before on a stick of Liquorice.

They gazed anxiously at Mary Poppins, waiting for her to make up her mind.

"No borrowing or lending in this Nursery, please," she said tartly. "I will pay for one ride each. And one is all you will have." She swept from the room carrying the tray.

They stared at each other.

"What can be the matter?" said Michael. It was now his turn to be anxious. "She's never paid for anything before!"

"Aren't you well, Mary Poppins?" he asked uneasily, as she came hurrying back.

"Never better in my life!" she replied tossing her head. "And I'll thank you, if you please, not to stand there, peeking and prying at me as if I were a Waxwork! Go and get ready!"

Her look was so stern, and her eyes so fiercely blue, and she spoke so like her usual self that their anxiety vanished away and they ran, shouting, to get their hats.

Presently the quietness of the house was broken by the noise of slamming doors, screaming voices and stamping feet.

"Dear me! Dear me! What a relief! I was getting quite anxious!" said the house to itself, listening to

Jane and Michael and the Twins plunging and tumbling downstairs.

Mary Poppins paused for a moment to glance at her reflection in the hall mirror.

"Oh, do come on, Mary Poppins! You look all right," said Michael impatiently.

She wheeled about. Her expression was angry, outraged and astonished all at once.

All right, indeed! That was hardly the word. All right, in her blue jacket with the silver buttons! All right with her gold locket round her neck! All right with the parrot-headed umbrella under her arm!

Mary Poppins sniffed.

"That will be enough from you—and more!" she said shortly. Though what she meant was that it wasn't nearly sufficient.

But Michael was too excited to care.

"Come on, Jane!" he cried, dancing wildly. "I simply can't wait! Come on!"

They ran on ahead while Mary Poppins strapped the Twins into the perambulator. And presently the garden gate clicked behind them and they were on the way to the Merry-go-round.

Faint sounds of music came floating across from the Park, humming and drumming like a humming-top.

"Good-afternoon! And how are *we* to-day?" Miss Lark's high voice greeted them as she hurried down the Lane with her dogs.

But before they had time to reply she went on, "Off to the Merry-go-round, I suppose! Andrew and

Wulloughby and I have just been. A *very* superior
Entertainment. *So* nice and clean. And *such* a polite
Attendant!" She fluttered past with the two dogs
prancing beside her. "Good-bye! Good-bye!" she
called back over her shoulder as she disappeared
round the corner.

"All hands to the pump! Heave ho, my hearties!"

A well-known voice came roaring from the direction of the Park. And through the gates came Admiral Boom, looking very red in the face and dancing
a Sailor's Hornpipe.

"Yo, ho, ho! And a bottle of Rum! The Admiral's
been on the Merry-go-round. Bail her out! Cockles
and Shrimps! It's as good as a long sea voyage!" he
roared, as he greeted the children.

"We're going, too!" said Michael excitedly.

"What? You're going?" The Admiral seemed quite
astonished.

"Yes, of course!" said Jane.

"But—not all the way, surely?" The Admiral
looked curiously at Mary Poppins.

"They're having one ride each, Sir!" she explained
primly.

"Ah, well! Farewell!" he said in a voice that for
him was almost gentle.

Then to the children's astonishment, he drew himself up, put his hand to his forehead, and smartly
saluted Mary Poppins.

"Ur-rrrrrumph!" he trumpeted into his handkerchief. "Hoist your sail! And up with your Anchor!
And away, Love, away!"

And he waved his hand and went off rolling from side to side of the pavement and singing,

"Every nice Girl loves a Sailor!"

in a loud, rumbling voice.

"Why did he say Farewell and call you Love?" said Michael, staring after the Admiral as he walked on beside Mary Poppins.

"Because he thinks I'm a Thoroughly Respectable Person!" she snapped. But there was a soft dreamy look in her eyes.

Again Jane felt the strange sad feeling and her heart tightened inside her.

"What *can* be going to happen?" she asked herself anxiously. She put her hand on Mary Poppins' hand as it lay on the handle of the perambulator. It felt warm and safe and comforting.

"How silly I am!" she said softly. "There *can't* be anything wrong!"

And she hurried beside the perambulator as it trundled towards the Park.

"Just a moment! Just a moment!" A panting voice sounded behind them.

"Why," said Michael, turning. "It's Miss Tartlet!"

"Indeed, it is not," said Miss Tartlet breathlessly. "It's Mrs. Turvy!"

She turned, blushing to Mr. Turvy. He stood beside her smiling a little sheepishly.

"Is this one of your Second Mondays?" Jane enquired. He was right-side up, so she did not think it could be.

"Oh, no! Thank goodness, no!" he said hastily.

"We—er—were just coming to say—oh, Good Afternoon, Mary!"

"Well, Cousin Arthur?" They all shook hands.

"I wondered if you were going on the Merry-go-round?" he enquired.

"Yes I am. We all are!"

"All!" Mr. Turvy's eye-brows shot up to the top of his head. He seemed very surprised.

"They're going for one ride each!" said Mary Poppins, nodding at the children. "Sit still, please!" she snapped at the Twins, who had bobbed up excitedly. "You're not Performing Mice!"

"Oh, I see. And then—they're getting off? Well— Good-bye, Mary, and Bon Voyage!" Mr. Turvy raised his hat high above his head, very ceremoniously.

"Good-bye—and thank you for coming!" said Mary Poppins, bowing graciously to Mr. and Mrs. Turvy.

"What does Bon Voyage mean?" said Michael, looking over his shoulder at their retreating figures— Mrs. Turvy very fat and curly, Mr. Turvy very straight and thin.

"Good journey! Which is something *you* won't have unless you walk up!" snapped Mary Poppins. He hurried after her.

The music was louder now, beating and drumming on the air, drawing them all towards it.

Mary Poppins, almost running, turned the perambulator in at the Park Gates. But there a row of pavement pictures caught her eye and she pulled up suddenly.

"What is she stopping for now?" said Michael in

an angry whisper to Jane. "We'll never get there at this rate!"

The Pavement Artist had just completed a set of fruit in coloured chalks—an Apple, a Pear, a Plum, and a Banana. Underneath them he was busy chalking the words—

TAKE ONE

"Ahem!" said Mary Poppins, with a lady-like cough.

The Pavement Artist leapt to his feet and Jane and Michael saw that it was Mary Poppins' great friend, the Match Man.

"Mary! At last! I've been waiting all day!"

The Match Man seized her by both hands and gazed admiringly into her eyes.

Mary Poppins looked very shy and rather pleased.

"Well, Bert, we're off to the Merry-go-round," she said, blushing.

He nodded. "I thought you would be. They going with you?" he added, jerking his thumb at the children.

Mary Poppins shook her head mysteriously.

"Just for a ride," she said quickly.

"Oh——" He pursed up his mouth. "I see."

Michael stared. What else could they do on a Merry-go-round *except* go for a ride? He wondered.

"A nice set of pictures you've got!" Mary Poppins was saying admiringly, gazing down at the fruit.

"Help yourself!" said the Match Man airily.

And with that Mary Poppins, before their astonished eyes, bent down and picked the painted Plum from the pavement and took a bite out of it.

"Won't you take one?" said the Match Man, turning to Jane.

She stared at him. "But *can* I?" It seemed so impossible.

"Try!"

She bent towards the Apple and it leapt into her hand. She bit into the red side. It tasted very sweet.

"But how do you do it?" said Michael staring.

"I don't," said the Match Man. "It's Her!" He nodded at Mary Poppins as she stood primly beside the perambulator. "It only happens when She's around, I assure you!"

Then he bent down and picked the pear clean out of the pavement and offered it to Michael.

"But what about you?" said Michael, for though he wanted the Pear, he also wanted to be polite.

"That's all right!" said the Match Man. "I can always paint more!" And with that he plucked the Banana, peeled it, and gave half each to the Twins.

A clear sweet strain of music came floating urgently to their ears.

"Now, Bert, we must really be going!" said Mary Poppins hurriedly, as she neatly hid her Plum-stone between two Park railings.

"Must you, Mary?" said the Match Man, very sadly. "Well, Good-bye, my Dear! And Good Luck!"

"But you'll see him again, won't you?" said Michael, as he followed Mary Poppins through the Gates.

"Maybe and maybe not!" she said shortly. "And it's no affair of yours!"

Jane turned and looked back. The Match Man was standing by his box of chalks, gazing with all his eyes after Mary Poppins.

"This *is* a curious day!" she said, frowning.

Mary Poppins glared at her.

"What's wrong with it, pray?"

"Well—everyone's saying Good-bye, and looking at you so strangely."

"Speech costs nothing!" snapped Mary Poppins. "And a Cat can look at a King, I suppose?"

Jane was silent. She knew it was no good saying anything to Mary Poppins because Mary Poppins never explained.

She sighed. And because she was not quite sure why she sighed, she began to run, streaking past Michael and Mary Poppins and the perambulator towards the thundering music.

"Wait for me! Wait for me!" screamed Michael, dashing after her. And behind him came the rumbling trundle of the perambulator as Mary Poppins hurried after them both.

There stood the Merry-go-round on a clear patch of lawn between the lime trees. It was a new one, very bright and shiny, with prancing horses going up and down on their brass poles. A striped flag fluttered from the top and everywhere it was gorgeously decorated with golden scrolls and silver leaves and coloured birds and stars. It was, in fact, everything Miss Lark had said, and more.

The Merry-go-round slowed up and drew to a

standstill as they arrived. The Park Keeper ran up officiously and held on to one of the brass poles.

"Come along, come along! Threepence a ride!" he called importantly.

"I know which horse I'll have!" said Michael, dashing up to one painted blue-and-scarlet with the name "Merry-Legs" on its gold collar. He clambered on to its back and seized the pole.

"No Litter Allowed and Observe the Bye-Laws," called the Keeper fussily as Jane sped past him.

"I'll have Twinkle!" she cried, climbing upon the back of a fiery white horse with its name on a red collar.

Then Mary Poppins lifted the Twins from the perambulator and put Barbara in front of Michael and John behind Jane.

"Penny, Tuppeny, Threepenny, Fourpenny or Fivepenny rides?" said the Merry-go-round Attendant, as he came to collect the money.

"Sixpenny," said Mary Poppins, handing him four sixpenny bits.

The children stared, amazed. They had never before had a sixpenny ride on a Merry-go-round.

"No Litter Allowed!" called the Keeper, his eye on the tickets in Mary Poppins' hands.

"But aren't you coming?" Michael called down to her.

"Hold tight, please! Hold tight! I'll take the next turn!" she replied snappily.

There was a hoot from the Merry-go-round's chimney. The music broke out again. And slowly, slowly the horses began to move.

"Hold on, please!" called Mary Poppins sternly.

They held on.

The trees were moving past them. The brass poles slipped up and down through the horses' backs. A dazzle of light fell on them from the rays of the setting sun.

"Sit tight!" came Mary Poppins' voice again.

They sat tight.

Now the trees were moving more swiftly, spinning about them as the Merry-go-round gathered speed. Michael tightened his arm about Barbara's body. Jane flung back her hand and held John firmly. On they rode, turning ever more quickly, with their hair blowing out behind them and the wind sharp on their faces. Round and round went Merry-Legs and Twinkle, with the children on their backs and the Park tipping and rocking, whirling and wheeling about them.

It seemed as if they would never stop, as if there were no such thing as Time, as if the world was nothing but a circle of light and a group of painted horses.

The sun died in the West and the dusk came fluttering down. But still they rode, faster and faster, till at last they could not distinguish tree from sky. The whole broad earth was spinning now about them with a deep, drumming sound like a humming top.

Never again would Jane and Michael and John and Barbara be so close to the centre of the world as they were on that whirling ride. And somehow, it seemed, they knew it.

"For—— Never again! Never again!" was the thought in their hearts as the earth whirled about them and they rode through the dropping dusk.

Presently the trees ceased to be a circular green blur and their trunks again became visible. The sky moved away from the earth and the Park stopped spinning. Slower and slower went the horses. And at last the Merry-go-round stood still.

"Come along, come along! Threepence a ride!" the Park Keeper was calling in the distance.

Stiff from their long ride, the four children clambered down. But their eyes were shining and their voices trembled with excitement.

"Oh, lovely, lovely, lovely!" cried Jane, gazing at

Mary Poppins with sparkling eyes, as she put John into the perambulator.

"If only we could have gone on for ever!" exclaimed Michael, lifting Barbara in beside him.

Mary Poppins gazed down at them. Her eyes were strangely soft and gentle in the gathering dusk.

"All good things come to an end," she said, for the second time that day.

Then she flung up her head and glanced at the Merry-go-round.

"*My* turn!" she cried joyfully, as she stooped and took something from the perambulator.

Then she straightened and stood looking at them for a moment—that strange look that seemed to plunge right down inside them and *see* what they were thinking.

"Michael!" she said, lightly touching his cheek with her hand. "Be good!"

He stared up at her uneasily. Why had she done that? What could be the matter?

"Jane! Take care of Michael and the Twins!" said Mary Poppins. And she lifted Jane's hand and put it gently on the handle of the perambulator.

"All aboard! All aboard!" cried the Ticket Collector.

The lights of the Merry-go-round blazed up.

Mary Poppins turned.

"Coming!" she called, waving her parrot-headed umbrella.

She darted across the little gulf of darkness that lay between the children and the Merry-go-round.

"Mary Poppins!" cried Jane, with a tremble in

her voice. For suddenly—she did not know why—she felt afraid.

"Mary Poppins!" shouted Michael, catching Jane's fear.

But Mary Poppins took no notice. She leapt gracefully upon the platform, and, climbing upon the back of a dappled horse called Caramel, she sat down neatly and primly.

"Single or Return?" said the Ticket Collector.

For a moment she appeared to consider the question. She glanced across at the children and back at the Collector.

"You never know," she said, thoughtfully. "It might come in useful. I'll take a Return."

The Ticket Collector snapped a hole in a green ticket and handed it to Mary Poppins. Jane and Michael noticed that she did not pay for it.

The music broke out again, softly at first, then loudly, wildly, triumphantly. Slowly the painted horses began to move.

Mary Poppins, looking straight ahead of her was borne past the children. The parrot's head of her umbrella nestled under her arm. Her neatly-gloved hands were closed on the brass pole. And in front of her, on the horse's neck——

"Michael!" cried Jane, clutching his arm. "Do you see? She must have hidden it under the rug! Her Carpet-bag!"

Michael stared.

"Do you think——?" he began in a whisper.

Jane nodded.

"But—she's wearing the locket! The chain hasn't broken! I distinctly saw it!"

Behind them the Twins began to whimper but Jane and Michael took no notice. They were gazing anxiously at the shining circle of horses.

The Merry-go-round was moving swiftly now, and soon the children could no longer tell which horse was which, nor distinguish Merry-Legs from Twinkle. Everything before them was a blaze of spinning light, except for the dark figure, neat and steady, that ever and again approached them and sped past and disappeared.

Wilder and wilder grew the drumming music. Faster and faster whirled the Merry-go-round. Again the dark shape rode towards them upon the dappled horse. And this time, as she came by, something bright and gleaming broke from her neck and came flying through the air to their feet.

Jane bent and picked it up. It was the gold locket, hanging loosely from its broken golden chain.

"It's true, then, it's true!" came Michael's bursting cry. "Oh, open it, Jane!"

With trembling fingers she pressed the catch and the locket flew open. The flickering light fell across the glass and they saw before them their own pictured faces, clustered about a figure with straight black hair, stern blue eyes, bright pink cheeks, and a nose turning upwards like the nose of a dutch doll.

"Jane, Michael, John, Barbara and Annabel Banks,
and
Mary Poppins."

read Jane from the little scroll beneath the picture.

"So that's what was in it!" said Michael, miserably, as Jane shut the locket and put it in her pocket. He knew there was no hope now.

They turned again to the Merry-go-round, dazzled and giddy in the spinning light. For by now the horses were flying more swiftly than ever and the pealing music was louder than before.

And then a strange thing happened. With a great blast of trumpets, the whole Merry-go-round rose, spinning, from the ground. Round and round, rising ever higher, the coloured horses wheeled and raced with Caramel and Mary Poppins at their head. And the swinging circle of light went lifting among the trees, turning the leaves to gold as the light fell upon them.

"She's going!" said Michael.

"Oh, Mary Poppins, Mary Poppins! Come back, come back!" they cried, lifting their arms towards her.

But her face was turned away, she looked out serenely above her horse's head and gave no sign that she had heard.

"Mary Poppins!" It was a last despairing cry.

No answer now came from the air.

By now the Merry-go-round had cleared the trees and was whirling up towards the stars. Away it went and away, growing smaller and smaller, until the figure of Mary Poppins was but a dark speck in a wheel of light.

On and on, pricking through the sky, went the Merry-go-round, carrying Mary Poppins with it. And

Away it went and away, growing smaller and smaller

at last it was just a tiny twinkling shape, a little larger but not otherwise different from a star.

Michael sniffed and fumbled for his handkerchief.

"I've got a crick in my neck," he said to explain the sniff. But when she was not looking he hurriedly wiped his eyes.

Jane, still watching the bright spinning shape, gave a little sigh. Then she turned away.

"We must go home," she said flatly, remembering that Mary Poppins had told her to take care of Michael and the Twins.

"Come along, come along! Threepence a ride!" The Park Keeper, who had been putting litter in the baskets returned to the scene. He glanced at the place where the Merry-go-round had been and started violently. He looked around him and his mouth fell open. He looked up and his eyes nearly burst out of his head.

"See here!" he shouted. "This won't do! Here one minute and gone the next! It's against the regulations! I'll have the law on you." He shook his fist wildly at the empty air. "I never saw such a thing! Not even when I was a boy! I must make a report! I shall tell the Lord Mayor!"

Silently the children turned away. The Merry-go-round had left no trace in the grass, not a dent in the clover. Except for the Park Keeper, who stood there shouting and waving his arms, the green lawn was quite empty.

"She took a Return," said Michael, walking slowly beside the perambulator. "Do you think that means she'll come back?"

Jane thought for a moment. "Perhaps. If we want her enough," she said slowly.

"Yes, perhaps . . . !" he repeated, sighing a little, and said no more till they were back in the Nursery . . .

"I say! I say! I say!"

Mr. Banks came running up the path and burst in at the front door.

"Hi! Where's everybody?" he shouted, running up the stairs three at a time.

"Whatever is the matter?" said Mrs. Banks, hurrying out to meet him.

"The most wonderful thing!" he cried, flinging open the Nursery door. "A new star has appeared. I heard about it on the way home. The Largest Ever. I've borrowed Admiral Boom's telescope to look at it. Come and see!"

He ran to the window and clapped the telescope to his eye.

"Yes! Yes!" he said, hopping excitedly. "There it is! A Wonder! A Beauty! A Marvel! A Gem! See for yourself!"

He handed Mrs. Banks the telescope.

"Children!" he shouted. "There's a new star!"

"I know——" began Michael. "But it's not really a star. It's——"

"You know? And it isn't? What on earth do you mean?"

"Take no notice. He is just being silly!" said Mrs. Banks. "Now, where is this star? Oh, I see! *Very* pretty! Quite the brightest in the sky! I wonder where it came from! Now, children!"

She gave the telescope in turn to Jane and Michael and as they looked through the glass they could clearly see the circle of painted horses, the brass poles and the dark blur that ever and again whirled across their sight for a moment and was gone.

They turned to each other and nodded. They knew what the dark blur was—a neat, trim figure in a blue coat with silver buttons, a stiff straw hat on its head, and a parrot-headed umbrella under its arm. Out of the sky she had come, back to the sky she had gone. And Jane and Michael would not explain to anyone for they knew there were things about Mary Poppins that could never be explained.

A knock sounded at the door.

"Excuse me, Ma'am," said Mrs. Brill, hurrying in, very red in the face. "But I think you ought to know that that there Mary Poppins has gone again!"

"Gone!" said Mrs. Banks unbelievingly.

"Lock, stock and barrer—gone!" said Mrs. Brill, triumphantly. "Without a word or By Your Leave. Just like last time. Even her Camp-bed and her Carpet-bag—clean gone! Not even her Postcard-album as a Memento. So there!"

"Dear, dear!" said Mrs. Banks. "How very tiresome! How thoughtless, how and—George!" she turned to Mr. Banks. "George, Mary Poppins has gone again!"

"Who? What? Mary Poppins? Well, never mind that! We've got a new star!"

"A new star won't wash and dress the children!" said Mrs. Banks crossly.

"It will look through their window at night!" cried Mr. Banks, happily. "That's better than washing and dressing."

He turned back to the telescope.

"Won't you, my Wonder? My Marvel? My Beauty!"
he said, looking up at the star.

Jane and Michael drew close and leant against him,
gazing across the window-sill into the evening air.

And high above them the great shape circled and
wheeled through the darkening sky, shining and
keeping its secret for ever and ever and ever . . .

CELEBRATING

YEARLING

25 YEARS

Yearling Books
celebrates its
25 years—
and salutes
Reading Is
Fundamental®
on its 25th
anniversary.